PRINCESS OF INDEPENDENCE

ICARUS BOBAIN

CONTENTS

CRISTINA, NEW YEAR'S DAY, 1848

Milan

Giovani's salon boasted few furnishings: a lone sofa against one side of the room, a liquor cabinet and a counter on the other. In contrast to his always ornate and extravagant dress, his home was modest in appearance. Though he often hosted parties, his guests were made to stand, lest they get too comfortable and linger past their welcome. For his more intimate gatherings—and it was through those that he made his reputation—his guests would sit on floor cushions before inevitably opting to lie on the plush carpets, which were softer than a bed and just as practical for the intentions of Giovani. The emptiness of the space made me feel anxious. Without the armrests of a chair to grip or a table to set my drink on then pick back up, thus keeping my hands in near constant motion, I found myself instead, pacing and pulling at my skirts.

Francesco, who was sitting on the sofa, followed me with his eyes and mimicked my nervous habit by gripping his trousers at the knees and pulling on them, stretching them then letting go so they'd release with a snap. He made a game of imitating me, and it was a game I was not in the mood for.

I went to the window to gaze down at the piazza at the merchants stirring below, but standing there motionless was only making me more and more anxious. I turned from the window and gestured for Francesco to vacate the sofa, a request he took as an order which he quickly and obediently carried out.

"You've tired of watching the piazza?" said Giovani from the other side of the room, his back to me and his attention perusing the bottles of his liquor cabinet. "Not much of a show, is it?"

"Quite the opposite," I said.

The sofa was slanted in such a way that it was nearly impossible to sit on it straight. Instead, I rested my back against the arm rest and lay down, my legs dangling off the side where Francesco had taken up post at my feet like a lapdog tethered to me by a leash of his imagining.

"I never tire of watching the piazza," I said. "But as for the show—as you so vulgarly put it—it's the script that has me nervous."

"Not to mention the lack of any meaningful rehearsal," said Giovani. He pulled out a bottle, lifted it to the light and examined its contents.

Giovani had been instrumental in helping spread the message of the boycott, though I'd always known that to him it was but a game, or, as he so callously put it now: a show. While everyone in Milan, regardless of political affiliation or social status, was revolted, and justly so, by the incidents of last September where the police fired on a crowd that had gathered to honor the new Archbishop of Milan, Romilli, the responses people called for varied greatly. Some, like Giovani, at least initially, wished to rouse up the populace to take to the streets again, this time with far less peaceful intent. This kind of violent manifestation would have been good for his newspaper. Though he'd never admit to it, surely that had some influence on his way of thinking. I, on the other hand, had suggested against taking to the streets. I suggested that in order to free ourselves from the oppressive powers that ruled us and kept us divided, first we had to weaken their power by striking at the very source of that power: the finances.

I grew up with money; I was born into it, a vast fortune that had made me—at age sixteen and at the time of my wedding—the richest heiress in all of Italy. I had seen first hand, the power and influence that money could wield. And, when deprived of access to my finances and made to flee to Paris without any substantial means, I saw first hand how the absence of money can leave one powerless and easily subjugated, at the mercy of all and of any.

"We do not need to take up arms against the soldiers patrolling the streets," I'd said. "We need to deprive the state of its resources, deprive them of the means to finance the soldiers. We boycott tobacco and gambling, and we deprive the government of its means to impose its will. We boycott tobacco and gambling, and the ruling power is immediately and irrevocably weakened.

"Then, we'd need not take up arms against the soldiers,

but rather they'd turn their arms on those giving them orders. A state deprived of its finances is a state deprived of its soldiers. And a state deprived of its soldiers is a state deprived of its power.

"A change of power that is brought about through violence will lead inevitably to a governance driven by the need to maintain such violence. Whereas, a change of power brought about by an adjustment to economic balance will lead inevitably to a governance driven by the need to maintain such economic balance."

Giovani had published my essays; he had helped disseminate the message of the boycott, though I suspected he didn't really believe in it but had merely wanted to test its potency. It didn't matter much to me. Effective collaboration always interested me more than sincere collaboration. Some would argue that made me a cynic; others would argue I was a pragmatist. I would argue that I was both.

"You'll have another drink," said Giovani, his back to me as he closed the liquor cabinet with one hand and raised a bottle with the other.

"It's barely mid-afternoon," I said. "You'll have me drunk by sundown."

Giovani flashed me a smile and raised an eyebrow. "That's precisely the point."

"I'll pass. Thank you." I let my hand fall onto Francesco's head. I petted him lightly as I glanced back toward the window. The piazza was gone from view. At this height, from the top floor of the four-story building, I could see but the tops of the apartment buildings that stretched from the piazza into Porta Tosa and the surrounding suburbs of Milano.

Giovani turned to Francesco. "You'll join me, won't you, Francesco?"

"A man who passes on drink and would let his friend drink alone," said Francesco, "Is a man who will soon find himself without either."

"Well said." Giovani filled up Francesco's glass then he filled up his own. "What shall we drink to, Cristina? The boycott? The revolution? Italy free and prosperous?"

I did not find the condescension in his voice upsetting. I was used to it by now. Instead, I found it motivating. *The boycott will succeed in weakening the state. The revolution will be successful. Italy will be free. And Italy will prosper.*

"Why not drink to irony," I said. I pulled myself off the sofa and went again to the window.

"Irony?" Giovani asked.

I went to open the window but stopped and turned to him. "Do you not see the irony? A revolution of the people against the powers that hoard all the riches and use them to subjugate the masses, yet here we are, we who have worked tirelessly to stir the masses against such abuse—doing so by using the very riches we claim to be at the heart of the injustice. And we watch from high up on our perch, looking down at those who we've roused to do our bidding."

My discourse fell on silent and rather astonished looking men until Francesco turned from me, glanced at Giovani and said, "Sounds to me, less like irony and a bit more like hypocrisy."

Giovani, whose mouth had hung half open during my

discourse, now let it drop wide, his eyes opening wide as well. He turned to me and said, "My Princess, can you believe the tongue on this one?" He turned to Francesco then back to me. "I'd say that show of insolence deserves a spanking, wouldn't you?"

I chuckled. "I'll leave that to you and your firm hand, my dear Giovani."

I turned from them and opened the window. The cool air was refreshing on my face. It nipped a bit, which I found, at the moment, quite invigorating. Below, the merchants were enjoying a rare holiday, puffing on big cigars (the most ostentatious display of support of the boycott of state-taxed tobacco, since the cigars did not come from the heavily taxed Lombardia-Venetia region). They gathered in small groups of five or seven outside the closed doors of the various shops that lined the piazza. I could make out some familiar faces as well as the sounds of laughter and the occasional jeer thrown in the direction of a passing soldier.

Behind me, Giovani and Francesco made exaggerated sounds of slapping and pleading, no doubt meant to arouse my curiosity and turn me away from the outside view.

My curiosity was aroused, but it was not from their childish games. A group of merchants had joined themselves to another and were now taking turns marching back and forth in mockery of the Austrian soldiers watching them from nearby. Giovani's metaphor of 'a show' was being mirrored perfectly on the piazza, as it was a sort of theatre performance the merchants were giving, with three sets of spectators: one, the other merchants howling and cheering with laughter, the other three soldiers who watched with stiff postures and stern faces, and of course me, watching from the warmth and comfort of Giovani's salon, not unlike a gallery box at the opera.

"Cristina," Giovani sang-called to me. "You're missing all the fun."

Without turning to him, I replied, "Somehow I doubt that."

The soldiers stopped watching the merchants mocking them. They turned their backs on them and slowly walked away.

One of the merchants flicked the butt of his cigar toward the soldiers. It hit one of them on the head and bounced to the ground.

I stifled a chuckle.

The soldier turned to the group of merchants and said something I could not make out, though the tone was clear: not at all amused.

The merchant who had flicked the cigar smiled widely and offered exaggerated claims of innocence. Then the soldier turned from him and left.

"Cristina," Giovani called again, "what's the fun of putting on a show if there's no audience?"

I turned from the window and looked at him. He sat on the floor, legs spread wide. Francesco was laid out with his head resting on Giovani's crotch.

I offered Giovani a smile. "Why, Giovani, that's the first sensible thing you've said all day."

He and Francesco beamed from the approval. "Come, will you?" He gave the floor beside him a pat. "Why watch a spectacle, when you can be part of it?"

I cocked my head to the side.

"That's two sensible things I've said, isn't it?" he asked with a wry smile.

I nodded. "I believe you're right, Giovani." I turned back to the piazza and the scenes playing out there below.

"Cristina," Giovani called again. This time his voice carried with it a tone of petulance and impatience.

I sighed and left the window to the cheers and applause of both Giovani and Francesco.

"Gentlemen," I said to them, "and you'll admit I'm being most gracious with that term, I believe I will go down to the piazza for a spell."

Their smiles quickly vanished. "You'll what?"

"Do enjoy yourselves," I said as I walked by them. "I shall return when I'm hungry. You did promise me lentils." I furrowed my brow and wagged a finger at Giovani. "And you will come through on your promise, won't you?"

He frowned.

I smiled, put on a jacket, waved and walked out the door.

Somehow the piazza was colder than I had expected. I looked at the sky to see the sun already making its retreat into the horizon. I thought to return for a thicker jacket, but Mauro Carruglio waved to me from the corner.

"Cristina," he called out, his voice rising above the dozens of others competing in the piazza and down its side streets. "Auguri, Cristina!"

I walked briskly to him. Immediately, the spirit of the piazza overtook me, and I ceased to feel the cold. I even stopped myself from buttoning up my jacket, instead, letting my movement send the flaps to blow behind me like a sail.

"Auguri, Mauro!" I said before I had reached him.

"Auguri, Cristina," he responded with matching enthusiasm.

We embraced then he started to sing a song: a waltz even older than he was. He quickly forgot the words, but he continued humming, and he twirled me around to the tempo of his tune.

"Auguri," said his son, Luigi.

"Auguri, Luigi."

We were a dozen; and we danced and we celebrated. Mauro offered me wine. I refused, politely, but he served me some anyway.

I was happy again. I loved the contradictions of New Year's Day: the lethargy of the body after a long night of long drinks, yet somehow full of energy from the celebrations of the first day of the year; the hopes of prosperity reigning the piazza shared by workers who were not at work and by merchants whose merchandise was not for sale on that day. I'd always found these kinds of contradictions stimulating. There was something about being pulled by opposing forces that no singular force, no matter how well focused, could compete with.

I thought of Francesco's comment from earlier: the 'hypocrisy' of the wealthy perched in their salon four stories above the piazza, looking down on the workers they were trying to mobilize in an effort to strip the powerful of their wealth and thus strip them of their power. It was precisely this sort of contradiction that fueled our movement. It was precisely this sort of contradiction that was the motor to our revolution. I laughed to myself.

Mauro, though he didn't know the source of it, joined me in my laughter, and Luigi followed suit. We laughed without knowing why. But it was New Year's Day; there was no need to have a reason to laugh.

"Eighteen forty-eight will be our year, won't it, Cristina?" said Giusepi.

I smiled and nodded. There was too much joy and certainty on his face to entertain any thoughts of measured optimism. "Yes it will, Giusepi. Eighteen forty-eight will be our year."

"Auguri," he said, and he raised his glass.

"Auguri," I replied, and I raised mine.

The sun was gone; I had hardly noticed its exit. Evening came upon us with little warning. It was only then that I regretted the light jacket I was wearing. I sat on the steps of the newstand, huddled in my own arms. I looked across the piazza up at Giovani's salon. The window had remained open. I thought to leave to go fetch a warmer jacket. Even though it would take me mere minutes to leave and return, the salon seemed so far away and I stood and took my first step with much hesitation.

"Will you have some lentils with us?" said Mauro.

"Yes. Thank you," I said. "But first, I must go fetch a warmer jacket."

"Nonsense," said Mauro. "I will get you a blanket."

I opened my mouth to protest, but he was already gone, disappeared around the corner. Had I had the chance to protest, it would have fallen on deaf ears anyway. Mauro, Luigi and Giusepi alike, they were not ones to let a kind offer go unaccepted, especially not on New Year's Day.

The soldiers from earlier had returned, except they had been joined by three more of their comrades.

The group that had mocked them earlier were still gathered on the corner. They, too, were slightly larger in number, and slightly more inebriated and significantly louder.

The Austrian soldiers marched around the piazza, taking a path that was much closer to the sidewalk than their habitual path. They stared down the small group of men and women playing cards at an overturned crate that served as their table. The men stared back and sarcastically invited the soldiers to join them, with the promise that they would fleece them of the shirts on their backs. "We could use a tablecloth," said one of the card players. "How about a quick hand? Who knows, you might even win yourself a fine Italian cigar." He took a puff from his cigar and blew the smoke in the direction of the passing soldiers.

No doubt the soldiers didn't understand a word of what the card players were saying to them, but no doubt they understood the sentiment.

I felt a slight bit of pity for the soldiers. They understood they were being mocked yet were unable to understand the specifics of the insults being hurled at them. They weren't wanted; nobody was happy to see them; everyone wished they would just go away. The pity I felt lasted only a brief moment, as the soldiers inched closer still to the sidewalk while they continued their rounds. This could only have the effect of provoking the groups of people they passed, people gather merely to celebrate the new year.

The pity I'd felt then turned to anger. *Why don't you just go away? Or, if you absolutely must walk the piazza, at least have the good sense not to walk so close to the sidewalk.*

"Here you are, Cristina," said Mauro as he proudly wrapped a blanket around me. "And now a bowl of lentils and you'll be warmer than an afternoon in May."

"Thank you, Mauro. You're too kind."

Tradition would claim that for every lentil you eat on New Year's Day, you'll receive a lira during the coming year. And while no one actually believed this to be true, everyone still filled his or her bowl with lentils and ate with enthusiasm and optimism. It's funny how tradition often trumps belief or even common sense. In a way, it's quite reassuring. Our bowls were full of lentils just like we knew the coming year would be full of riches.

We didn't need common sense to know this was true; it was tradition.

As I ate, I watched the soldiers pass before another group who blew the smoke from their cigars in the faces of the soldiers. One of the soldiers sneered at them.

That wouldn't have happened if you'd maintained a reasonable distance.

When the soldiers had passed, Francesco di Cervelli, who owned a dairy shop in Port Tasa that reputed to have the best Mascarpone in Northern Italy, flicked his cigar butt in the direction of the soldiers. It bounced off the shoulder of one of them and landed at his feet.

The group laughed, and another man, though I

couldn't see exactly who, also flicked his cigar butt. It whizzed by a soldier, barely missing his cheek.

The soldier spun around and marched back toward the group, shouting something in German.

The group laughed again and proclaimed their innocence. The other five soldiers returned and managed to pull their colleague away from the confrontation.

"Tasty lentils, aren't they?" said Luigi as he came over to me with pot and ladle in hand.

It took me a moment to pull my attention from the soldiers and look over at Luigi. I smiled. "Yes, they are very good. Thank you."

He ladled out another serving and offered it to me. "Care for some more?"

I shook my head. "No, thank you." I set down my bowl, stood up and motioned to the soldiers. "This doesn't look good."

Just as the words left my mouth, another three cigar butts sailed through the air, from whose hands I couldn't be sure, and hit the soldiers on their heads and backs.

Two of the soldiers spun around and darted hostile glances from one small group of men to another.

"I don't know why they feel the need to patrol the piazza," said Mauro. "It's supposed to be a holiday."

Two of the soldiers stepped up to a group. The exchange was loud, but I couldn't make out any of the words as soldiers and merchants both talked over each other and in different languages.

"They don't eat lentils in Austria, do they?" said Mauro. "Why would they? They don't need to hope the riches will come. They've already got them; more riches than Italy's got lentils."

I walked over to the cluster of soldiers and merchants shouting back and forth. I had no idea what I would say or do; it was pure instinct that carried me there. Mauro followed me, and a few steps behind him, Luigi, the son, followed the father.

A few soldiers not involved in the dispute managed to pull their colleagues away just as I arrived.

"Auguri," I said. But there was little enthusiasm in my greeting. Instead, it sounded unintentionally more like a question.

"Auguri, Cristina," Francesco di Cervelli responded with no less apprehension.

We stood there, our small group of Mauro and his family and friends now joined with Francesco di Cervelli's small group. We exchanged timid greetings, all of our heads turned to watch the soldiers depart from the piazza toward the avenue Viale Bianca Maria.

We weren't the only group to have stopped our celebration to focus, instead, on the soldiers. Small clusters of men and women and children now spilled onto the piazza, all with their attention on the soldiers.

More than a few cigar butts pelted the soldiers as they made their retreat. Larger objects, too, were hurled at them: a slice of bread, a soggy vegetable.

The six soldiers stopped and turned to the piazza. The small clusters of people were uniting, forming larger groups. They raised their voices and walked toward the soldiers.

I wondered then if Giovani was watching from his

fourth-story salon. Would he, despite his callousness and cynicism, be concerned, just as I was?

I glared at the soldiers, who obstinately stood there facing the piazza. *You're nearly out of the piazza. Just turn and continue walking away. Just go. Leave already!*

Mauro put his hand on my shoulder. "Come on," he said. "Let's head back. This doesn't concern us."

I let myself be led back, but upon reflection and after a few paces, I turned to Mauro and said, "Then who does it concern?"

"Today, we celebrate the New Year," he said. "Tomorrow,"—he paused reflectively—"well, tomorrow the boycott will have sent the soldiers home, right?" He looked at me and smiled.

I smiled back, but I quickly averted his gaze and stared, instead, at my steps.

Again I took a seat on the step by the newsstand, wrapped the blanket around me again and took up my bowl of lentils. They were cold now. But even cold lentils promised riches.

I glanced across the piazza and up at Giovani's salon. The window was closed, and no lights shone from within. The sleep I'd been deprived of these last few nights suddenly and without warning caught up to me. I leaned back against the newsstand and thought I might doze off right there and then, on the step, in the cold evening surrounded by people cheerfully celebrating the New Year.

Luigi invited me to join in on their card game. I gladly accepted. I was not a superstitious woman, but I was faithful to my traditions: we mustn't fall asleep on New Year's Day before midnight.

I quickly lost myself in the game, in the banter and the laughter. Occasionally, I would take a glance at the piazza and at Viale Bianca Maria, but it appeared that the soldiers had gone and were finally leaving us alone.

"This time, I'll deal," I said to Mauro.

"Oh, but you can't deal as fast as me," said Mauro.

"Maybe not," I said. "But I also can't slip cards from the bottom of the deck." I winked at him.

"Cristina," he protested with a wry smile on his face, "I would never do such a thing."

"Of course you wouldn't." I stuck out my hand. "The cards, Mauro."

I shuffled. Luigi chuckled. "I believe, now, your luck will turn," he said to his father. "Of course that will be a mere coincidence."

"Luck!" Mauro protested. "It's not luck; it's skill."

As I dealt, the clamour of celebration around us increased. So did the number of people whisking past us. I stopped dealing and looked around.

"One more," said Mauro. "One more card."

I set the deck down and stood. "Something's happening."

A crowd had gathered near Viale Bianca Maria and more people were running towards it.

"Luigi," said Mauro, "get inside."

"But I…"

His protest faded out behind me, as I, without thinking, found myself walking towards the crowd, the clamour of which drowned out Mauro's calls for me to return.

Ahead of me, not more than a dozen paces, the crowd began to disperse. People ran left, smacking into others who were running right. Cries and shouts came from the front. Beside me, a young man I did not recognize, picked up a stone from the ground and he charged toward the scattering crowd.

"Wait," I said, and I ran after him.

A woman darted past me, pulling a young child behind her by the hand.

I turned to avoid them and someone smacked into me from the side, knocking me to the ground.

"Oh, I'm sorry, Cristina."

It was Gianni Boccaccio, the owner of the newsstand I had been sitting at earlier. He bent down and helped me up. "Come," he said. "We need to leave."

As he helped me up, I looked to my left and saw what everyone was running from. Soldiers, at least a dozen, possibly more, charged through the crowd. Some wielded batons, others wielded swords, others rifles, but they all aimed them at the people they were charging.

Gianni held onto my hand. He tried to lead me away from the crowd. I dragged my feet, but I did not pull away from his hold.

"What—" Before I could finish my exclamation, a soldier directly in my line of view thrust his sword into the side of a man who was trying to run away.

"No!" I yelled and jerked my hand free from Gianni's.

"Cristina!"

His call was already far behind me as I sprinted toward the man, now lying on the ground clutching his side. People zipped by me, bumping my shoulders, knocking me this way and that. I didn't lose sight of the man. One man tripped over him then pulled himself up and ran off.

Another man hopped over him while more frantic people ran around him looking over their shoulders and shouting.

When I was at arms' length from him, a woman ran into me from the side. I did not fall; I did not even stumble or break my stride. Without taking my eyes off of him, I pushed the woman out of my way and went to the wounded man.

"My goodness," I said. "Are you OK?"

He turned to me. I did not recognize him, but at the same time I knew him. He was Italian. He was a worker. He had been celebrating the New Year in the piazza. He had been eating lentils with the promise of riches to come. He was my fellow countryman, my neighbor, my friend.

"Can you stand?" I asked.

He grimaced and attempted to get to his feet. Blood poured liberally from his side despite his hand pressed against the wound.

I put my arms around him and lifted him to his feet. Somebody rushed by me and knocked into me from behind while someone else knocked into the wounded man causing him to teeter. "I've got you," I said. "Come with me."

I led him the best I could through the dispersing crowd toward Mauro's shop. I caught a glimpse of Luigi standing against the door on his tiptoes scanning the crowd. "Luigi!" I called out.

He looked around frantically, but he didn't see me.

The man gasped and groaned.

"Hold on," I said. "We're almost there."

With one arm holding him up and the other out in

front of me shielding us from the chaos of people running every-which-way, we made it to Mauro's shop. "Luigi."

"Cristina! Are you all right?"

"Open the door, Luigi."

He rummaged in his pockets and retrieved a set of keys. He fumbled with the lock then, at the sound of a loud agonising cry, he turned to look back at the crowd.

"Luigi, open the door!"

He unlocked the door and pushed it open. "I lost sight of my father," he said.

I pushed past him into the small aisle whose shelves were adorned with seeds and spices. The wounded man let out a muffled cry of pain. I eased him onto the floor and knelt at his side.

He looked at me and said, "Are you a nurse?"

I turned to Luigi. "Get me a knife, a candle and matches."

I looked back at the man. "Let me see where they got you."

I pulled up his shirt. The wound was deep, and it stretched from the base of his ribs and wrapped around his flank to end at his waist. Already a pool of blood was forming around my knees; my dress, like the man's shirt, was drenched.

"I'm going to cauterize your wound," I said matter of factly. "Do you understand?"

He groaned, laid back and set his head on the floor, turning it from me.

"Will these do, Cristina?"

I turned to Luigi who held out an ordinary kitchen knife, a long thin candle and a box of matches. "That's perfect, Luigi. Now, light the candle and set it down, here, beside me.

As Luigi executed my orders, I addressed the wounded man. "Try to pinch the wound closed." I put my hand on his blood-wet skin and pinched. "Like so. Can you do that for me?"

He didn't respond. His hands moved across his belly slowly.

"What's your name?" I asked.

"Enzo."

I took his hand and guided it towards his wound. "Stay with me, Enzo. You're going to be all right. But I need your help right now." I took his thumb and index finger and helped him pinch the upper part of his wound. "I need you to hold that tight. Can you do that?"

"Yes."

I had never cauterized a wound before, but I had heard tales. In Paris, a friend of Francois had told us of a hunting accident he had been witness to and how he had to cauterize a wound in the middle of the forest. I hadn't believed his story at the time. He was constantly telling stories, each one more outlandish than the last. But at that moment, kneeling beside Enzo who was bleeding out in the aisle of Mauro's shop, his story was the only instruction I had to go by. I did exactly as Francois's friend told us he had done.

I heated the knife by the candle's flame until the knife turned black. Then I laid the blade against the wound and kept it there for a few seconds.

Enzo didn't cry. He didn't shout or curse. Instead, he mumble-hummed a song I didn't recognize. It sounded like the kind of song men would sing at the pubs to lament the passing of better days.

"You're very brave, Enzo," I said.

He turned to me finally and said, "And you are an excellent nurse."

2

MARIA, 1848

Paris

There was a confectionery shop on Rue de Rivoli we would always go to after school, Mirielle and I, accompanied by Mirielle's mother, Madame Desclos. Mother always left me money for a treat, but I would use that money to buy candy for Mirielle. Some days she would choose fruit jellies, other days she would choose nougat. On the days she chose fruit jellies, she would share them with me, though I never asked. It never occurred to me to offer Madame Desclos anything from the shop; after all, it wasn't Madame Desclos's attention I was trying to secure.

I wonder, now, looking back on that time in my life, whatever became of Mirielle. Had I set an unhealthy precedent? Did she grow up always expecting her affection to be bought with regular gifts and bribes? Or, unlike me, was she able to eventually make friends based on common interests and mutual respect?

I never did return to Paris after the short time I spent there as a child. Though my husband spoke often of taking a holiday there; he had friends and business acquaintances in Paris; it would have been perfectly natural and we would have been perfectly at home spending a summer there. I would always suggest another city, another land for our holidays. And my husband would always take my suggestions.

Paris has a special place in my heart, and not necessarily a particularly favorable one. We had a beautiful home, my mother and I, on Rue de Castellane, one block behind l'église de la Madeleine. From the outside, it looked like nothing out of the ordinary. In fact, its small windows looking out into the cramped courtyard offered little exterior evidence of the vast space and simple, yet elegant style of our home's interior. On a few occasions, Mirielle would walk home with me, but I would not invite her in. Given the humble exterior and the deplorable state of the courtyard, I bet she thought I was ashamed of my home, ashamed of my family's modest stature.

The truth was, in fact, quite the contrary. We lived well, and my mother often hosted soirees with very important people and much admired artists and musicians. The truth was, that my mother was almost always home. And I wouldn't invite Mirielle in, because I knew that with just a few minutes of her company, Mirielle would become fascinated with my mother; she would like and admire her just like everyone else liked and admired her. Then all the tales I'd told of my mother's callousness and cruelty—accurate tales in the eyes of my eleven-year-old self at that time—would then lose their credibility to

Mirielle, who was, in truth, my only friend and the only one I confided in.

My mother wasn't like other mothers I'd met. She treated everyone the same, whether servant or banker or politician; she addressed them as her peers, regardless even of their age. Within a few minutes, she would have had Mirielle feeling like an important grown-up conversing about history and politics with another important grown-up who was her equal. How then could Mirielle possibly understand me when I'd complain about my mother? Who then would be my confidant with a sympathetic ear? To be treated like a grown-up conversing with her equal, for Mirielle that would have been great. But for me, when could I be treated simply like a little girl? Why must I be bothered with news of politics and revolutions sweeping across Europe? Where were my fairy tales, my princesses with magical powers, my knights in shining armour?

If I'd had those growing up, perhaps I would have been more tolerant of my mother's frequent talk of a free and unified Italy, of economic equality and her frequent rants about corruption in government. But even my governess, Mlle Courbe, focused her lessons on the empire and new waves of political thinking and struggles for liberation across Europe. I wanted none of it.

I did, though, try my hand at art. My mother provided me with an excellent teacher, Mlle Dubois. I would paint mostly plants and flowers, and I was getting pretty decent at it for a girl of eleven years of age. Yet, the drawing room was full of my mother's canvases: people sitting at desks, soldiers with rifles raised above their heads, dreadfully boring stuff. Her canvasses leaned against the walls, watching me as I worked on a still life; a basket of tangerines, I remember, had been the last painting I attempted. Stern-looking men with a plume in hand, stern-looking soldiers with a sword or rifle in hand all looking out at me from their canvassess, all had my mother's severe eyes.

I tired of painting, and the basket of tangerines went unfinished.

I fared better with my music instruction. There was no politics or revolution in music, at least none that I could perceive at that age. Mother would invite the greatest pianists of Paris and all of Europe to entertain in her salon. One in particular, I remember well: Maurice Dietrich. I don't recall what he had played for us, but I do remember the feeling it gave me. I was transported, no longer in a stuffy salon in Paris, no longer surrounded by boring men talking about boring things. I was carried away by clouds whose touch tickled my arms and my cheeks. I was warmed by gentle rays of sun while a cool breeze blew the hair from my eyes.

Maurice was dreamy. A handsome man, perhaps not in a conventional sense, but he had a handsome soul that shone through him and permeated the room. After his performance, he bowed and he looked my way. I must have blushed for days.

Paris should have been a happy time for me: with our large house always bustling with people, the music, the arts, the walks in the gardens with Mirielle and the confectionery shops. But the spectre of Italy always loomed over me. How could it not? Mother talked of Italy constantly. I always knew we would go back. I always knew that the comforts and the beauty of Paris were temporary; a cruel trick to play on a young child, to show her a world of wonders and gaiety while at the same time reminding her constantly that they would be taken from her at any moment.

The memories of Italy I'd brought with me to Paris were no doubt corrupt, filtered through the eyes of a naïve and careless little girl. I remembered mostly our home: the front door that was too heavy for me to open easily; the curved staircases whose steps were too far apart so that I had difficulty climbing them and I was constantly told to move more quickly; the strong smell of herbs that lingered in the entranceway and mixed with that of mildew and rotting wood.

I remembered also my mother's visitors, always in a hurry, unlike the men and women she'd receive in Paris, who would enter our home with a lazy air. They'd exchange polite greetings and speak of the pleasantness of the day. I was allowed, even encouraged, to participate. The visitors would ask me about my lessons then share their memories of their own lessons, the ones they'd always claimed to have forgotten. It wasn't until the aperitifs had been leisurely consumed and the glasses and plates cleared that I would be taken away by my governess so that the adults could enter into their adult conversations. In Italy, the guests would arrive in a flurry of commotion. Their greetings would be quick and they'd lack the flair of the Parisians' exaggerated formalities. The guests would speak fast and with wild hand gestures, without waiting for me to be escorted away by my governess.

While I was too young at that time to understand the

specifics or even to have developed trustworthy notions and memories, for me, as a young girl in Paris, Italy was chaos and anxiety: chaos and anxiety we had fled, but a chaos and anxiety I always knew we would return to inevitably.

My mother, of course, would speak of Italy in far more favorable terms. She would often color her French with an Italian turn of phrase and lament the lack of such a phrase in French. She would compliment the cook on a particular dish then quickly recall a similar one she'd had in Italy whose quality could not be replicated elsewhere for lack of the great Italian herbs, meats and vegetables.

In an effort to instill in me the same kind of longing nostalgia for Italy my mother felt, a few short months after we'd settled in Paris, once the charm of the city had me in its spell, my mother bought me a doll, a painted porcelain doll of a young Italian girl dressed in a traditional costume of Sardinia: red skirts covered in the front with a embroidered green apron; an open vest with ornate designs decorating its long sleeves; and covered with a red hood that draped her shoulders.

"Her name is Bella," said my mother, "and she is from Tertenia in Sardinia. Before the big feast, Bella will come down from the hills. She'll go to the beaches and dig up clams. Then she brings them home to her parents. Her mother will be rolling fregola, little beads of pasta, and then together they'll prepare a delicious seafood fregola for the feast. Everyone from the village and surrounding villages comes and tastes the delicious seafood fregola, and they bring drinks made from the grapes of their vines. And everyone sings, and everyone dances. She's beautiful, Bella, don't you think?"

I did think my doll was beautiful, but I didn't like her name.

"I'll call her Belly," I said.

Mother laughed. "Belly is not a name for a young girl from Sardinia."

"She's not from Sardinia," I said. "She's from Normandy." I cradled the doll in my arms and turned my back on my mother so that her eyes couldn't fall on the doll. "And her name's not Belly; it's Belly Belly!" I stomped loudly and defiantly to my room.

A few weeks went by before Mother brought up the subject of the doll. One evening at supper with no preamble or segue, she inquired, "How's Belly?"

It took me a moment to grasp who or what she was asking about, since I had put the doll at the bottom of my toy chest, covered it in a blanket and had forgotten about it since. "You mean Belly Belly?" I said.

Mother frowned. "Yes. How is she? Are the two of you getting along?"

It was only years later, as a mature woman, that I could look back on that peculiar suppertime conversation and understand that mother was asking about my feelings for Italy. Had I adjusted to my new, albeit temporary, life in Paris? Had I adjusted too well and had I, as she suspected, forgotten my native land?

At the time, I only understood that she was asking me about my doll. I even suspected that she was jealous of it, since she had spoken so glowingly about it, and I had hidden it from her.

"She's fine," I said. "She has been collecting apples for her mother's tarts and her father's cider. Always collecting apples; that's Belly Belly."

"Not digging for clams?" said Mother.

I shook my head.

I could see this answer disappointed her, and I was glad.

A few months later, and again I had forgotten all about Belly Belly when again Mother brought up the subject over supper. "Tomorrow, we are receiving three fine gentlemen from Nuoro. Nuoro is a province of Sadinia, where Belly is from."

I glanced up from my plate and looked at my mother with suspicion. She rarely told me who we would be receiving and when she did so, she never used words such as 'fine gentlemen'.

"I think these gentlemen would love to meet Belly," she continued. "Do you think Belly could make an appearance? Perhaps we could set her on the mantle. She would be comfortable there, don't you think?"

For the entire time we'd been in Paris, I was angry at my mother for dragging me into her boring, messy adult life, making me talk to the boring, yet supposedly important adults she'd entertain in her salon. I was angry at her for not recognizing I was but a child and wanted to indulge in carefree childish things. Yet during that supper, finally she spoke to me as a child, and I despised her for it.

I didn't know who these 'fine gentlemen' were or why they would possibly be interested in my doll, whose name was not Belly, but Belly Belly. But I did know—and with absolute certainty—that Belly Belly wanted no part in spending an evening in their company.

"Unfortunately," I said in a matter-of-fact tone of voice, "Belly Belly won't be available this evening. She has to prepare for a big party. Her friend, her best friend, Juliette, is having a birthday. She will be turning fifteen. It will be a big party. Everyone in Normandy will attend. So naturally Belly Belly will be quite busy helping her mother with the tarts and helping her father with the ciders, not to mention dressing all the tables and tending to the horses."

"Is that so?" said Mother. "I'm very sorry to hear that. Maybe I could have a talk with Belly and—"

"Her name is Belly Belly!"

"Do not interrupt your mother, young lady." Mother straightened in her chair and smoothed out her skirts like all the women did in Paris when they were upset or when they were about to say something upsetting. "Perhaps I could have a talk with Belly Belly. Maybe she will want a break from her work. And maybe she will want to spend a few hours in the company of people from her home country."

I could not protest any further. After supper, mother went with me to my room. She stood at the doorway and waited for me to hand over my doll.

I pulled her out of the bottom of my toy chest, from under the blanket where I had hidden her away to be forgotten. I combed her hair and smoothed out her dress then I gave her over to Mother.

"You keep her locked away in the chest?"

"The chest isn't locked," I said.

Mother stayed at the doorway for a long moment. I turned my back to her and straightened the objects on my desk. Finally, when the weight of our silence had me struggling to remain standing, she said, "Thank you. I will give her back to you after the morrow. I just want these gentlemen to see her. You understand?"

"Yes, Mother."

The following afternoon, I was especially cheerful and kind to my mother in the hope that she would not have me escorted into the drawing room with my governess but rather I would be allowed to meet my mother's guest and perhaps gain some understanding as to how a child's doll could be of interest to them. My efforts paid off, as Mother invited me to stay with her so that we could greet her guests together.

They were older men, Italian, but dressed in the fashion of Paris. They spoke to us in my native Italian, yet I had to struggle to understand them. Fortunately, I was not called upon to say much.

While they took their aperitifs, Mother showed them various books and paintings she had set about the salon. Apparently, this had been done specifically for these men and quite recently too, for I knew Mother's salon well and I had never seen those particular books or paintings before. "This will be His Eminence," she said as she directed their attention to a canvas that had been propped against the far wall. "I've commissioned the painting from a brilliant young painter, Vincenzo Abrami. He is originally from Rome. I'm putting him to good use after I found him wasting his talents on French gardens."

Mother's guests laughed at this comment. At that moment, I did not think them very 'fine' at all.

"You can see in the crowd, this young man is from Umbria," she continued, "and here beside him is another man from Romagna. When it is finished, all of Italy will be presented. All of Italy will be united in this gathering."

"Very fitting," said one of the guests, nodding his approval.

"It will be a fine work," said the other guests.

"And you will surely recognize this," said Mother as she passed from the painting over to the mantle where Belly Belly stood.

I hadn't even noticed her there, next to the silver candle holders. She blended in with all the other trinquets Mother had arranged to show her guests, transforming the once lively salon into a dull museum.

"Oh, my. Would you look at that," exclaimed one of the guests.

"I had her brought over from Cagliari, though I believe she was made in Siniscola, which I believe is not far from your home, is that true?"

"Precisely," said the guest, visibly delighted. "She could very well be my neighbor."

Mother handed Belly Belly to the man. He examined her dress, examined her hair, turning her in his hands while my own hands balled into fists. I had to bite down on the insides of my cheeks not to shout at him. *Get your hands off of her. Put her down. She is not your neighbor. She is Belly Belly, and she's from Normandie, not Italy!*

He passed Belly Belly to his friend and said to my mother, "I am so homesick, you know."

Mother nodded. "As am I."

"Though I must be away from my beloved Italy," the man continued. "Raising the funds we need would not be possible if we had stayed, as you are no doubt aware."

Again, Mother nodded.

The guests thanked her for her generosity, and for a moment I thought she was giving these men my doll. But Mother returned Belly Belly to the mantle place and led them to a chest of drawers from which she pulled out a series of letters. She did not look at me, and I felt forgotten sitting there in my chair. I glanced over my shoulder at the doors hoping my governess would come for me, but the doors did not open. I coughed, hoping to draw my mother's attention so she would see me and realize I was sitting there neglected, then I could ask to be excused.

My coughs went unnoticed, so I sat quietly looking from the doors to my mother and her guests. They spoke of money. And the only sense that I gathered was that Mother was giving them a substantial amount, and the men were grateful. The money was to be used in Italy but it would have to pass first through many hands. Their conversation made me even more anxious to leave. Though, at the time, I understood little of what they were talking about, I did get the clear sense that it was not meant for my ears, or for anyone's ears but theirs for that matter.

After some talk, my mother handed one of the guests the packet of letters she'd shown them. Then, the guest slipped them into the inside pocket of his vest. He turned from my mother, and his eyes met mine.

I was stiff with fear, and I forgot how to breathe.

The man smoothed over his vest and he smiled at me. "Don't worry, little girl. You will be back in Italy soon, very soon."

"Maria," Mother said to me, "where is your governess?"

I could not respond. I could not even take my eyes off the man who continued looking at me, and he continued smiling.

"Why don't you look for her?" Mother suggested. "She may be in her quarters. If not, maybe you could do your reading in your room. Would that be OK?"

I blinked and swallowed. The man took his eyes off of me and I was able to turn to my mother. "Yes. Yes I will do that."

"Very well. Thank you, Maria."

I hopped off my chair, ran to the mantle, grabbed Belly Belly and ran out the doors and straight to my room.

We endured a particularly rude winter that year. I spent most of my days indoors. But I didn't mind. I took more and more music lessons and actually became quite accomplished at the piano. I even played my études for my mother's guests at a few of her soirees. It did not bother me that other pianists would play after me, all of whom were accomplished artists, the very best in Europe it was often said. They played their music and it was spectacular. But my études were special; they had been written specifically for me by my instructor Louis Alain.

During one such musical soirée, after I had played for the guests and received a polite round of applause, one of the guests—a portly man with a distractingly long moustache—addressed the pianist who had come to entertain us. He attempted to cajole the musician into trying his hand at my études. "Let us hear what you can make of those simple melodies," he said. "I do believe with your mastery you will be able to turn them into quite an extraordinary piece of music."

The pianist politely refused, but the guest insisted and eventually the pianist acquiesced to the guest's demand.

"May I?" the pianist said to me.

I had no right to refuse and didn't know how to even if I had been so brash.

He took my sheets, placed them on the stand and took his seat at the piano. He played the first few bars just as I had played them but then his fingers slowed and his notes became unsure. He stumbled his way through the next few bars then stopped. He turned to the guest who had insisted he play my études, and he said, "I apologize, but these études are quite difficult. I would need to work hard on them before attempting to perform them."

He handed me back my sheets, bowed slightly and said to me, "Congratulations. You certainly do have a lot of skill, young lady."

I smiled then put my hand over my mouth to hide just how giddy I was at that moment. Of course, I knew he was merely being kind and flattering. But it still felt good, nevertheless.

After that exchange, he returned to the piano and regaled us with his music which was of a beauty and grace that surpassed any of the music I'd ever heard before in Mother's salon.

Years later, when I was a grown woman vacationing with my mother in Turkey, she asked me if I remembered that evening.

I told her that yes, I remembered.

"Do you remember the name of that pianist?" she asked.

I shook my head no.

Mother smiled wide and took a slow sip from her aperitif before telling me. It turned out that the pianist who had humiliated himself in order to flatter me, a little girl of eleven years of age, was none other than Valentin Alkan, whose greatness was rivaled only by his kindness.

The harsh winter we endured that year carried over into spring. When finally, in the mid weeks of April, warmer and sunnier days began to drive the cold and gloom away, all of Paris took to the parks and the sidewalk cafes. There was a sense of hope and optimism sweeping through the city; 'the worst is behind us; better days lie ahead.'

However, that sentiment stayed away from our home. Mother did not have time for leisurely walks in the garden nor did she have the temperament for enjoying a lazy afternoon at the cafes. Instead, she received more and more men and women from foreign lands—more and more Italians especially. They met with nervous excitement. The conversations were shorter, more hurried, more panicked. There were no aperitifs or light snacks or gentle conversations about the weather.

I gathered bits and pieces of conversations I heard between my mother and her guests. I learned that the Pope had left Rome, and for some reason, this meant that we would have to leave Paris. I asked my governess if this was true. She said she didn't know about these things, but she told me that things were changing in Europe, and changing fast.

"But why do we have to leave Paris?"

My governess said that I should ask my mother. I did, hoping that she would tell me that I had misunderstood, that we weren't going to leave Paris, that we would stay there forever and be happy. But she didn't say anything like that. Instead, she said that this was a great chance for Italy, that Italy needed her and that we would be leaving in the coming weeks.

I was angry at my mother, and I was angry at Italy.

My governess helped me pack my things. I had meant to leave Belly Belly behind, but my governess found her in the kitchen pantry where I'd hidden her and she brought her to me. "We nearly forgot to bring Belly Belly with us."

"I don't want her," I said. "Put her back in the pantry."

Later, Mother spoke to me. "Maria, if you don't want Belly Belly, I would very much like to have her. I think she's a beautiful doll."

"No, I want her!" I exclaimed.

"Very well, Maria. I will pack her with your spring dresses, since your other dolls and books are already on their way to Italy. That means she'll be travelling with us. How does that sound?"

"Fine," I said.

Later that day, when everyone was busy preparing for supper or busy making final arrangements for our departure, I unpacked Belly Belly. I snuck her away into the garden of the courtyard and buried her under the ivy.

3

CRISTINA, 1849

Rome

I was only six years old when Napoleon's reign came to an end, too young to understand the event but not too young to be spared its consequences. The demise of the French empire led to the return of Austrian rule in Northern Italy. Napoleon had been defeated, however the revolutionary spirit he had awakened in men and women throughout Europe had not. My stepfather, the Marchese Alessandro Visconti d'Aragona, whom I loved dearly and who had raised me and cared for me and my mother ever since my father's passing, was one such man. He was passionate about politics and even became a leader of the Liberal party in Lombardy. He ensured I received an education, not only rich in letters and the arts, but also in the patriotic spirit of the Carbonari: anti-clerical and democratic, thus fiercely feared by the ruling class.

When the Austrians returned to Northern Italy, they

immediately set out to eradicate the families of those that had caught the fervour of the French revolutionary ideals. They came for my stepfather. Though he was more fortunate than most, having been spared execution, he was nonetheless jailed. I cannot know the horrors he suffered at the hands of his Austrian jailors, though I witnessed their lingering effects. He returned to us a tired, sick, beaten-down shell of the vivacious and caring man I had known as a child.

My mother reacted to this tragic turn in fortunes by taking on a lover—a penniless libertine of high-standing Sicilian ancestry. She made little effort to hide her indiscretion, and her and my stepfather's marriage, like my dear stepfather's health, degenerated quickly and dramatically before my very eyes.

For the constant unease and tension that kept ours from being a happy home, I blamed my mother as much as I blamed the Austrians. I vowed not to make the same mistakes she had, mistakes born from selfishness and vanity. Though, good intentions are no protection against the caprices of the heart; I would make my own mistakes in love and marriage, and like my mother, my conscience was troubled little by the consequences.

I was fifteen, and Prince Emilio Barbiano di Belgiojoso was twenty-three. I was not the only young girl in Milan to pine for him. Blessed with a glorious voice, which, combined with the charms of his education, earned him the adulation and admiration of all of Milan. Unlike his peers, he cared little for his appearance, letting his hair grow out, letting it wave and curl as it wanted. Free from the constraints of vanity, he carried with him a carefree alure rivalled only by the kindness that shone in his soft eyes.

My family was opposed to our marriage. They cited his libertine reputation and his knack for accruing debt as reasons for me not to marry him. Their protests had no sway on me. My heart was set on its prince.

Prince Emilio had not accrued debt from games or from vice, but from his generosity, for he was incapable of coming upon a troubled soul and not giving what he could to help. His generosity extended to those Italians forced into exile by the Austrians—a regular expense I was more than happy to indulge.

I was not naïve. I knew that it was my inheritance that he was attracted to and not me. Yet, I adored him, and what good is an inheritance if it cannot satisfy a yearning heart. We married and spent our honeymoon in the palace of his ancestors, the Palazzo Belgiojoso in Merate.

Even though our marriage did not last, when I reached the age to collect my inheritance I paid off my ex-husband's debts, and gladly so—a kindness he did not repay me when, still in possession of my dowery, he could have helped me in those first troubled years in Paris when the Austrians prevented me from accessing my funds.

Instead, I sold what jewellery I had managed to take with me to Paris, and much of that money went back to Italy, to fund the militias and armies that were being formed in Sardinia, in the Papal States, in the Two Sicilies, and in all the lands in between.

"Your generosity is extraordinary," said Giuseppe, "extraordinary, perhaps to a fault."

I straightened and placed my hands flat on the table. I had been comfortable leaning back in my chair, thinking that Giuseppe had invited me over for more amicable motives; however, if he was going to criticize me, I was going to face him sitting straight, head up, shoulders back. "We need allies wherever we can find them," I replied.

He winced and set down his glass of wine, as if my comment had soured his drink. "Cristina, we need allies who have power."

I shook my head. "Again, my dear Giuseppe, you are mistaken. My need is to empower our allies, not the other way around."

He chuckled. "You're sounding more and more like 'them'."

This time it was I who winced. By 'them', I knew he meant those who married their revolutionary spirit with the ideas expounded by Karl Marx. Giuseppe made no attempts to hide his disdain for Marx. In fact, he'd often go out of his way to steer the conversation toward his German counterpart, then offering his critique of what he deemed was the championing of an over simplistic and unrealistic ideal.

Karl Marx, was enjoying a lot of success with his publications. His ideas of valuing the working class and restructuring society and governance accordingly were gaining in popularity throughout Europe. I suspected there was a certain amount of jealousy that fueled his hatred. Marx was more popular, and his popularity appeared to come about, seemingly, overnight, unlike

Geuseppe who'd been publishing for decades with limited success.

"Stirring up the masses, like Marx does," he continued, "that can only lead to chaos. That's not what I want for Italy."

"It's worked pretty well for France," I said.

Giuseppe looked at me from the corners of his eyes and he frowned. He stood from the table. "I want you to do me a favor," said Giuseppe.

"So you didn't invite me over simply to express your disapproval of my friends?"

He smiled at me. "I hardly think my approval, or disapproval, as the case may be, would have any sway over you." He walked briskly to his writing desk. "But, on the other hand, your approval..." He took a sheet of paper from his desk and waved it in the air like a flag. "I've written a letter to the Roman pontiff."

I put a hand over my mouth to hide the smile, but I was not quick enough to stifle a small chuckle.

Giuseppe looked at me sharply. "He needs allies more than ever, now."

"I remind you, you said the same thing a year ago."

Giuseppe set the sheet back down on the desk. "It was true then, and it's true now."

I had upset him; I could see the hurt in his eyes. Giuseppe was a proud man, perhaps a bit stubborn and unyielding at times, but that was part of his strength. I walked over to the writing desk and set my hand on his arm. "And what is this favor you want to ask of me?"

"I haven't sent the letter." He opened a drawer, pulled out a blank sheet and set it down next to the other. "As you have insinuated, yes, it's true, I have sent letters in the past, letters that received no response. But now, the Pope is in a dire situation."

I pulled my hand away and stepped back. "And you want to come to his aid?"

"With conditions, of course," said Giuseppe. He took out a plume and handed it to me.

I refused. "This is why you invited me here?" I might have felt disappointed if I hadn't been expecting such a request from Giuseppe. Nevertheless, I feigned to be hurt. "And I thought you were only interested in my money."

"I am very interested in your money. And so is, I suspect, the Roman pontiff. You'll admit, a letter coming from your hand carries more weight than any letter I could write."

I turned to him and smiled. "Flattery will earn you my appreciation, but it will not sway my convictions." I walked back to him. I did not take the plume from him. Instead, I touched him gently on the back of his hand. "I am not going to write any letter to the Pope or to any other member of the church. I am not going to write any letter to the king or to any other member of the court."

I took the plume from him and set it down then I took him by the hand and pulled him away from the desk. "How many letters have you written, Giuseppe, letters that have gone unanswered? Don't you see? We aren't going to change the power from within. The change must come from the outside, from the people."

"Now, you really sound like 'them'." He picked up the plume then tossed it back down. "You sound like you've been believing your own—"

"Shh." I put my index finger to his lips. "Let's not fight, Giuseppe. I'll be leaving soon. Let's not part with harsh words."

"Leaving? Where to?"

"Back to Milan, of course. You are right about one thing, it will carry more weight coming from my own hand. But I'm not talking about letters. We're past the point of writing eloquent words, spinning meek requests. I'm talking about action."

Giuseppe grabbed the sheet off his desk and raised it in his fisted hand. "This is action!"

I put my hand gently on his wrist and lowered his hand. "I'm talking about *real* action, real 'roll-up-your sleeves', 'put your hands in the dough' action. From here in Paris, all my efforts go from my hands and are transferred by the hands of another. You are right, it would carry more weight coming from my own hand. I need to go back to Italy."

Rome

Pope Pius IX fled Rome for the security of Gaeta, a fortress in the Kingdom of the two Sicilies. In Rome, which had been left without any local governance, popular assemblies formed. And since the Pope continued to project a safe return to Rome, he forbade Catholics from taking part in these assemblies, which he called 'Assemblies of the Damned'. The voting assembly which convened on February 9, 1849, was thus, highly republican. Naturally, it proclaimed the Roman Republic and promised, among other measures, lower taxes, a secular education, and freedom of the press.

The assembly also asked me to take an organizational position in the new republic. I offered to take on the direction of military hospitals and called upon other women in Italy to help me. I don't know if Florence Nightingale was kept informed of the work I was doing in Rome or if it was merely a coincidence that, four years later, she would mimic my volunteer corps of military nurses in her famous campaign in Crimea.

We set up and staffed twelve fully-functioning hospitals in a matter of days. And we did not have to wait for the beds to fill up with wounded soldiers.

While my dear friend, Countess Clara Maffei, received artists and poets in her salon—the rendez-vous place for all of the literary and artistic life in Milan—I stayed in my hospitals, at the bedsides of men who gave their lives for their country.

"Surely, you can pull yourself away from your duties for one night," said Clara. "This Friday, Victor Emmanuel, the prince of Piedmont no less, will be in attendance."

"I'm sure it will be a fantastic ball, but, alas, it is one I will have to miss."

Clara did not hide her disappointment, though I could not know if she lamented my absence or if she lamented the realization that her balls were not a top priority.

"It will be good for you," she said. "And bring Maria, naturally."

"Ah, Maria." I sighed and shook my head. "Poor child.

She is surely having a difficult time adjusting to her new environment."

"A child needs to dance and play." Clara smiled at me. "So does a grown woman from time to time."

I nodded in agreement.

"Furthermore, and for practical matters," Clara continued, "a dance could go a long way to smoothing over the discord."

"What discord?"

Clara didn't respond straight away. Instead, she kept walking at a leisurely pace, staring at her feet as she stepped.

"Clara, what discord?"

She jerked her head up at me as if snapped from her reverie. "Oh, you know. The prince and his father, they view you as a republican."

"I am a republican."

She smiled politely. "And a bit of a socialist one, too." She put her hands up defensively. "Not that I fault you for it."

"Please, Clara, you don't need to beat around the bush, not with me."

"Very well, Cristina. If you must know."

"You brought it up," I said. "And now that you have, you might as well come out with it."

She picked up her pace as if a fast walk would help her with the uncomfortable words. I had been on my feet for days and had been sleeping very little, but I did not ask her to slow down.

"I didn't go unnoticed that you weren't invited to King Charles's ceremony."

"I've been busy," I said.

Clara glanced at me from the side and smirked. "Be that as it may, what kind of friend would I be if I didn't make some kind of inquiry as to the reason for this omission?"

"I don't know. A less nosy friend?" She frowned, so I nudged her in the side. "Clara, that was a joke."

She didn't laugh. "You can joke and call me nosy. But you should have been invited, and you weren't. So I asked around. I asked why that was."

"And?"

"Well, like I said, you're seen as the socialist republican."

"I am a socialist republican."

"That's going to keep you from getting invited to balls."

I laughed. "What are they afraid of? That I'll come escorted by blacksmiths and shoemakers? That I dare share the king's wine with his lowly subjects?"

"Yes, Cristina," she said in a matter of fact tone of voice. "That's exactly what they're afraid of."

I stopped and pondered this. Clara stopped a few paces ahead of me and looked back, hands on her haunches.

"You know, Clara, that actually sounds quite fun, don't you think?"

She shrugged her shoulders.

"Maybe I will come to a ball," I said, almost to myself. However, I glanced at Clara and saw her eyes open wide. I smiled and put up my hand, palm out. "Not your ball, of course, but Armand Marrast is having a ball in a fortnight. I've no doubt you've received your invitation?"

She nodded.

I smiled a devious smile. "Perhaps, I will make an appearance."

Rome

A wounded soldier, a boy of only seventeen who volunteered his life for his country, gave up his last breath during the night. I had held his hand in mine just the day before. I had read to him from Dickens and had promised to resume the story the next evening. Yet he would die without having heard how the story ends, neither the one penned by Dickens nor the one written, in part, with his own blood.

I sent the sheets to be washed, and dressed the bed with new linens. No sooner had I made the bed than it was taken by another wounded soldier, another boy who'd answered the call of his country. The deaths accumulated and repeated in similar fashion, but none were ordinary. I slept little, during the bombing of Rome. I stayed in my place among the wounded, overcome by fatigue. I looked for that condition where you can forget everything, that condition which is called sleep. Yet how could I sleep when I knew that upon waking I would not find all those who had wished me a quiet night with a weak voice? I reluctantly let go of a hand to take hold of another. Yet, how could I predict which hands I would take for the last time? And as I made the beds, how could I know if the sheets I prepared would soon end up upside down on the pillow announcing a new martyr?

There were reports that Austria was attempting to sign an armistice, but with whom? The Piedmontese army was the largest, but with Garibaldi and his volunteers and soldiers sent from Tuscany, there were simply too many factions for Austria to negotiate with. The very fact that Italy was so strongly united in spirit and patriotism yet so weakly united in governance spelled an impossibility for any cease fire.

Reinforcements were sent to defend Piedmont. Rome was left vulnerable, and I prepared the beds to welcome Italy's sacrifice.

4

MARIA, 1849

Rome

$\mathcal{I}$ had heard many fantastical tales of the beauty of Rome: Greek gods carved out of rock stand before pools of cascading waters. Cobblestone streets wind past trattorias where fresh produce is on display in a rainbow of colors. Rising from the vast piazza is an Egyptian obelisk where the rivers of the known world become statues of stoic marble.

Yet, despite the many wonders that had been described to me, when we arrived in Rome I would see none of them. The weather was fair, still in the throes of winter, but it was a mild winter and it was nearing its end. But it was not the weather that kept me from exploring my new city.

'You will be safe inside,' I was told. 'It's only temporary, but there is too much unrest in the streets for us to venture out.'

'Temporary', at my age, meant a few days, but my mother had a much different interpretation of the word.

"Good morning, Maria." My governess appeared at my door. In contrast to the sing-song tone of her voice, she wore no signs of gaiety on her face. She was nineteen years old, but an old nineteen, as if, in the midst of her youth, she was already regretting it slipping away from her. I too felt my youth slipping away. Already, I longed for the strolls in the parks of Paris, the cakes and the madeleines consumed without care or worry over struggles and politics. I dreaded seeing the face of my governess. 'When I'm nineteen, will I look like her, too?' I dared a glimpse at her then shuddered and quickly averted my gaze.

"I see you are dressed and ready for your lessons," she said.

"Yes, Governess." Her name was Sylvia, but I called her Governess. She was the second governess I'd had since arriving in Rome—the first barely lasted three weeks—and since I suspected this new one wouldn't last long either, I never bothered calling her by name.

"I'm wearing a thick wool shirt under this pullover. If the weather is warm and I can take off the pullover, I won't be cold."

My governess frowned. "You won't need it. You'll be having your lessons in the drawing room today."

"But you promised!" I huffed and stomped my feet. "Yesterday, you said we would do our reading in the park."

She nodded. "I know, but—"

"And you promised!"

"Yes, but it's not safe to go outside. I'm sorry."

I crossed my arms and pouted. "Why isn't it safe?"

"You know why, Maria."

"You say that every time. 'You know why, Maria.' I don't understand why I can't go outside!" It was petulant, certainly, but I was in a childish mood and wanted her to experience my frustration.

She crossed her arms and sighed. "There is fighting in the streets because there is a revolution happening, child. The Austrians and the Vatican are fighting against Italians because they don't want to see a unified country. Perhaps you should be paying more attention in your classes."

"That has nothing to do with me," I said with a glare.

"You are right; their war has nothing to do with you. However, I'm charged with keeping you safe, and the fighting on the streets is unpredictable and dangerous, so we will not be going out today.

"Now get your books. Come along. We've already lost precious minutes."

I did not get my books. I did not move, not even to uncross my arms. "What's so precious about the minutes?"

My governess sighed loudly then she approached and put an arm around me. "I know you're upset, Maria, and I'm sorry I cannot keep the promise I made to you yesterday. But if we do our reading inside today, I promise that as soon as it's safe to go out, I will take you to the park, to many parks and to the piazzas."

"It's not fair," I said.

"I know it's not fair," she said, and she seemed to be speaking more to herself than to me.

"I didn't do anything wrong." I shrugged her arm off of me, and I stomped over to my writing desk, grabbed my books and stormed out of the room.

I had committed no crime in Paris that I should be punished for, yet swiftly and with little warning everything had been snatched from me: my friends—though I had few, they were all left behind in Paris—my home, which the apartment we stayed in in Rome could not pretend to rival. Even the simple pleasures of the cold wind on my face and my feet kicking at blades of grass, they had all been taken from me.

In the drawing room, I opened my book to the page my governess said, but I did not read.

"Shall I start, then?" said my governess.

I did not respond. Instead, I pursed my lips and fixed my eyes angrily on the page.

She cleared her throat and began to read. "La chiusa della strada—"

"Stop!" I said. I stood from my chair and walked out of the room.

"Where are you going? You haven't been excused!"

I hurried down the corridor and back to my room. I dug through the contents of my toy chest and retrieved a book. It was a book on the life of Johan Sebastian Bach, a gift from a pianist who had played in our salon in Paris. I had already read the book, and though I didn't think much of the story, it was the only book I possessed that was in French. I cradled it in my arms and hurried back to the drawing room.

My governess intercepted me in the corridor. "What is the meaning of all this?" she said quite indignant.

I didn't answer her but instead returned to my seat at the desk in the drawing room.

My governess also returned to the drawing room. She

closed the doors behind her and stood, her back to them, as if I were a prisoner she was meant to guard. I might as well have been a prisoner for all the freedom I was deprived of.

"Please, Maria," she said. "Would it be possible to get through our reading without any further incident?"

I opened the book indiscriminately, to the middle, chapter six. "Le jeune compositeur quitta donc sa ville native."

I did not take my eyes off the page, but I heard the stomping steps of my governess come quickly toward me.

"Il n'avait que sa passion—"

"What are you reading?" She stood behind me, her breath falling on my head.

"It's a book about the life of Johan Sebastian Bach," I replied.

She took the book from me. "We're not reading this today."

"But I—"

"I don't even speak French," she said. "How am I supposed to help you with your reading if I don't even understand the language you're reading in?"

She closed the book and put before me, again, the ugly boring book I had been staring at earlier: the book with the ugly boring words in that ugly boring language.

"We'll finish our reading of the two Sicilies," she said. "You can read about Sebastian Bach in your own time."

"It's Johann Sebastian Bach," I corrected.

"So it is."

I crossed my arms and curled my lips, but I did not read.

We sat a long moment in silence until my governess finally uttered a soft plea, "Please."

Though her voice was soft, it carried with it all the frustration and fatigue and exasperation she was surely feeling at that moment. However, her frustration and exasperation could not match mine. What did she know? She had never been to Paris. She didn't even speak French, nor had she ever left Italy. She could not understand the cruelty of the fates I was suffering under.

I glanced at her and saw a tired old woman. Her hair was poorly combed. The complexion of her skin was dull, and I was further angered.

"Please, Maria," she repeated. "Don't make me have to tell your mother."

I snapped at her. "And what would you tell my mother?"

"I would tell her that her bright, though sometimes mischievous, daughter refused to do her reading."

It wasn't much of a threat. I saw my mother rarely during those first few months in Rome. And when I did, she was too tired or occupied with her worries of the hospital to devote any concern for my lessons.

"I'll do my reading in French!" I said, far more loudly than I'd intended. The volume of my voice surprised my governess and it surprised me, too.

When she regained her composure, she folded her hands neatly on her lap and said in a soft voice, "But, Maria, you speak such beautiful Italian."

"There is no such thing as beautiful Italian," I said under my breath.

"Oh, my!" She raised her hands in the air, stood from

her seat and turned in half circles. "What words have fallen on my poor ears!"

I took, again, the book on the life of Johann Sebastian Bach and, again, opened it to chapter six. "Le jeune compositeur quitta donc sa ville native…"

Rome:

My governess—my second governess in Italy—stayed on past the three weeks I'd expected her to last. She put up with my occasional protestations, and she never did tell my mother about my occasional disobediences. She continued to promise to take me to the gardens and the piazzas, but the promises remained unfulfilled. On a particularly grey day in early March it rained just enough to wet the grounds I gazed at from my bedroom window, yet not enough to provide the comforting pitter patter that so perfectly accompanied my melancholy dreams. When my governess called for me to begin my lessons, I said to her, "One of these days I will have to go out and see this Italy everyone has told me is so magical. Even if they fight in the streets or perhaps because of it. I want to see just what it is they are fighting over."

"Someday soon, I promise," she said. "I've heard the soldiers are concentrating on the eastern side of the city. Maybe we'll be able to take a little tour of the western parts. Maybe even later this week. We'll see. I hope so, but I don't know."

The following day, she greeted me in my room with a bright smile on her face. I had dressed for another drab day indoors, but upon seeing the happy expression she wore, I headed straight for my wardrobe to change.

"Good morning, Maria."

"Good morning, Governess."

I pulled out my favorite jacket: sky-blue with pretty white lace on the cuffs. "Is it warm enough for this jacket, you think?"

The smile on my governess's face vanished immediately. She shook her head and stepped into my room. "We're not going outside today."

"But—"

She put a hand in the air, open palm out. "Don't be upset. I have good news."

I dropped my head and frowned. "I don't want good news. I want to go outside."

"How about going to a ball?" Her eyes widened and a smile reappeared on her face.

"A ball?"

"With music and dancing and ladies in pretty dresses and men in smart costumes."

I put the jacket back in my wardrobe. The idea of attending a ball, my first in Italy, was indeed exciting, but I didn't want to let my excitement show. I didn't trust my governess. She was always making promises she couldn't keep.

"Mr. Armand Marrast, the President of the Second Constitutional Assembly of France, is throwing a ball tonight."

I kept my head down. I didn't want to look at her. With the enthusiasm in her voice, I knew if I caught her eyes, I wouldn't be able to contain myself either, and I would, despite myself, express my own enthusiasm.

"And we're invited!" She took my hands and pulled me to her. "It's going to be the biggest and best ball Italy has ever seen. Aren't you excited?"

Finally, I looked at her. She was beaming, and I could no longer stifle my own smile from breaking out. "A ball with French men and French women?"

She nodded. "And Italian, of course. Mr Marrast is an important man so there will be many important people there,"—she smiled—"important people like you and your mother."

"And there will be dancing?" I asked.

"Of course, there will be dancing. And music. And—" She put a hand to her head and turned in half circles as if just remembering an important detail. "Mr. Russo is coming today to help you with your piano. Who knows? Maybe you will be asked to play a piece for the host."

I, too, beamed and turned in half circles. "Oh my. I am not ready." I looked for my sheet music but then remembered I'd left it in the music room. I took my governess by the hand and pulled her toward the door. "Come on. To the music room. I have so much practicing to do."

I spent hours practicing. Mr. Russo, my piano instructor, said he had never heard me play better. After several attempts, my governess finally managed to coerce me out of the music room. "We need to get dressed," she said. "I've laid out your yellow dress. Come." She extended her hand. I took it, and she led me back to my room.

I stood staring at the yellow dress. I had said that it

was my favorite, not only because of the soft yellow which reminded me of a sunny morning, but because of the matching floral pattern on the sleeves and collar. I liked the way they felt. When I'd get nervous, I could run my fingers over the floral pattern and trace the stems and the leaves.

"Well, don't just stand there," said my governess. "Let's get you out of those drab clothes and into this beautiful dress."

I shook my head. "I don't want to wear this dress."

"But—"

"I want to wear the blue dress."

The blue dress was not my favorite, but it was the most 'French'. It was made by a couturier in Paris, and it bore the same blue as the Paris flag with matching red cuffs and red collar.

Though my governess would not be attending the ball, she did ride in the carriage with me. My mother was having a dress made and we rode to the couturier's atelier to pick her up. The curtains were drawn on the carriage windows. When I went to open them, my governess took my hand and placed it back on my lap. "Not yet," she said, and I understood she meant there was still too much ugliness in the streets I wasn't ready to see and that I shouldn't look.

I couldn't help but think about all the tales I'd heard of how beautiful Rome was. Yet, I had been there several months and wasn't even allowed to look out a carriage window. This contradiction made me angry, so to quell my anger I tried to concentrate on the music I would play and not think about how unfair my situation was.

When the horses came to a stop, my governess hurried me out of the carriage and into a building where from deep inside, from a room hidden beyond the tight entryway, escaped the voices of several women carrying with them a mix of merriment and agitation. We were led down a corridor cluttered with rolls of fabrics of all colors and into a dressing room.

My mother stood in the center of the room, surrounded by women admiring the dress she was showing off. My jaw dropped in disbelief. The dress she wore had a large red band flowing diagonally from her shoulder down to the waist. The upper part of the dress, minus the red band, was white while the skirts were green. She could have spared the couturier the trouble and simply wrapped herself in the Italian flag. The effect would have been the same.

My mother spied me watching her and said, "What do you think?"

My face turned red from embarrassment. Thankfully, the other women responded in my place, heaping praise on the couturier and on my mother.

We were joined in the carriage by three men who appeared to be dressed for a day's labor rather than for the biggest and best ball Italy had ever seen.

"Maria," said my mother, "this is Mauro. He makes shoes for horses. Isn't that wonderful?"

"How do you do?" I mumbled.

"Doesn't your mother look simply amazing in those colors?" said Mauro. He did not expect a response but instead looked at my mother and smiled.

"And this is Luigi and his brother Marco." She motioned to the two men sitting in front of me.

"How do you do?" I mumbled.

"You didn't get a chance to meet them," said Mother, "but Luigi and Marco are the ones who painted our music room. They did a splendid job, wouldn't you say?"

I nodded, but I kept my eyes fixed on my hands folded on my lap. 'House painters and blacksmiths—what kind of ball is this?' I wondered.

When the carriage stopped, we filed out, and in front of us was a veritable palace. High columns framed the wide front doors where valets attended to the arriving guests; stone statues stood guard beside the many windows that looked down on the courtyard; a line of carriages stretched around a large fountain, in the center of which the statue of a large, muscular man plunged his trident into the back of a serpentine sea creature.

"Wow," said Luigi. "Would you look at this!"

"Impressive, indeed," said Marco.

A pair of valets came to greet us. Mother declined their invitation to accompany us to the entrance, saying we would wait here for the rest of our party. She left the valets in an awkward limbo and cocked her head to look around the approaching carriage. "I think that's them," she said.

"That's quite a fancy carriage," said Mauro.

Mother chuckled. "No, not that one. The one behind it."

The valets looked as bewildered as I was. We exchanged sympathetic glances.

Mother waved a hand in the air. "Flavio, Roberto, over here."

The man stepping out of the carriage heard his name, looked around and upon spotting my mother nodded and waved back. I can't imagine how they'd managed to fit so many people in that carriage, but from it spilled out four men and four women who came over to us smiling and waving. One man was dressed in the costume of the national guard. Another resembled a day laborer like Mauro, while the women, though their dresses were pressed and their hair carefully coiffed, looked more like cooks and servants than they did attendees of Italy's biggest and best ball.

Mother made quick introductions with rapid hand gestures. I mumbled 'how do you do?' repeatedly until the introductions appeared to be finished, and mother led our motley group toward the front doors.

I dragged my feet, not knowing if I wanted to enter with my mother and her flamboyant and tacky dress or if I wanted to enter with the shoemaker or servants in our entourage. Mostly, I wanted to bury my head in embarrassment.

A lady took my hand. "Isn't this simply thrilling?" she said.

I glanced up at her. I was too confused to offer her back a smile, though hers was big and bright and stretched from ear to ear.

"I suppose you go to these kinds of balls all the time," she said, then she leaned over and whispered in my ear. "This is my first ball ever."

When she straightened, I saw behind her big smile and

behind the exhilaration emanating from her eyes that there was also more than a hint of nervousness. I squeezed her hand and smiled. "Yes, this is thrilling. It's going to be a great ball, the biggest and the best Italy has ever seen."

The inside of the palace was no less spectacular than its outward appearance had led us to believe. Each room we traversed was more spacious than the last, each adorned with the finest paintings and statues. From high ceilings, decorated with ornate murals, hung glass chandeliers, while below, weaving their way through groups of men and women dressed as if celebrating the birth of a king's heir, were servants in white gloves holding up silver trays of champagne flutes.

My mother never failed to swipe a flute from a passing servant and hand it to someone in our entourage.

"Cristina, it's so nice of you to come." The man who greeted her was tall and handsome with a thin moustache that framed a stiff upper lip. His dress was less ornate than that of the other guests but made from the finest of materials. His impeccable French had me suspecting that this man was our host. For reasons I didn't completely grasp at the time, I feared him, and instead of presenting myself at my mother's side and requesting an introduction, I hid behind the strange common woman I had entered with, who seemed to be more interested in the champagne she was sipping than the distinguished French gentleman my mother was talking with.

"I see you've brought guests," he said. His eyes passed over us, and though we were sorely underdressed and out of place, I was unable to gleam any condemnation or insult from his expression. "Welcome," he said to us collectively, "I'm happy you could make it."

My mother introduced Mauro and Luigi to him with much enthusiasm. "One day you will have to come to my music room, and you will see the fantastic work they have done," she said. "It is people like Mauro and Luigi who make Italy beautiful, wouldn't you agree?"

"I wouldn't dare disagree with you, Cristina," said our host, and he extended a hand to Mauro then to Luigi.

The women pushed up against Mauro and Luigi, eagerly awaiting their turn to be introduced. I stood there feeling quite exposed, gripping nervously my rolled-up sheet music in my hands. Fortunately, I managed to duck from behind one woman to behind another, and I was spared being seen by the Frenchman.

"What do you think of my dress?" asked my mother.

He paused a moment before responding. "Well, it's very Italian. We can agree on that."

"As it should be," said my mother with a wry smile.

"I've heard of wearing one's politics on one's sleeve," said the Frenchman, "but you've taken it a step further, haven't you?"

This made everyone laugh, but I didn't understand why. Instead of easing the tremendous embarrassment I was feeling, the laughter only made it worse.

'If this is the biggest and best ball Italy has ever seen,' I thought, 'I don't want to ever attend another—at least not with my mother.'

Rome

The weeks following the ball, the weather improved and, I suppose, so did the fighting in the streets lessen, as I was granted more and more freedom to leave the stuffy confines of our home and take frequent strolls through the parks. The main points of the city that were purported to be so spectacular, as well as the River Tiber, were still forbidden to me. However, since I doubted more and more the claims of their beauty, I didn't much mind being deprived of the chance to see them.

I even found the parks to be ugly. They only reminded me of the beautiful gardens we'd left behind in Paris. And instead of helping to improve my mood, they merely further aggravated the resentment I harbored for my mother for tearing us away from Paris and bringing me into this battle zone of Rome.

"Does this mean the fighting will soon end?" I asked my governess as we walked leisurely through the park.

The expression on her face showed me she didn't quite understand my question. "I mean, we're going outside more and more often. Does that mean they'll stop fighting?"

"I don't know, Maria," she said quite solemnly. "I hear the Austrians have their hands full in Hungary. They won't be able to fight us forever."

"When they do stop fighting, will I be going back to France?"

She looked down on me with a furrowed brow. She, who had only known Italy, couldn't possibly understand what I was missing.

I had not been raised in the church, nor had I been taught any prayers, but I did know how to look up at the sky and wish with all my heart. This I did regularly, whether walking in the park or looking out the window of my bedroom, I wished for the fighting to end. Not because, like my mother, I wanted Italy to be free from foreign occupation, that I wanted Italy to become self-governing and democratic, but simply because I believed it was the fight that brought my mother here, and in consequence me with her. And I believed in my foolish twelve-year-old heart that once the fighting stopped, we would return to Paris and to the gay life we'd led there before.

With the exception of during those brief walks in the park, my relationship with my governess continued to sour. She dismissed Mr. Russo and put a stop to my piano lessons—the only lessons I truly loved. This was in response to my continued insistence on not doing my readings in Italian. I had only one book in French, and that was the only book I read from. I missed my piano lessons, but I wouldn't give in. If I'd inherited anything from my mother—and I suspect I did inherit quite a few traits—most notably would be her stubbornness. Once I had made up my mind or set my heart on a particular notion, no punishment or promised prize would deter me.

"How was your day today?" asked Mother over supper. "I hear you went to the petting zoo. That must have been exciting."

"It was fine," I said.

"Just fine?"

"Mother, when are we going back to Paris?"

"Perhaps in autumn."

"Really!?" This was not the first time I had asked such a question. But it was the first time I had received anything close to a positive response. I lit up, almost jumped right out of my seat.

"Sure," said Mother. "Why not? We could spend a week or two in Paris, visit the old sites, old friends. That would do us good."

She knew I wasn't asking about a holiday. I was crushed and angry. "May I be excused?"

"Is something the matter? You've hardly eaten."

"I have no appetite."

That night I lay in bed staring at the ceiling, and I wished with all my heart to be back in Paris. That's not all I wished for, though. I'm ashamed to admit it, but I was only a child, an angry, lonely and confused child. That night I wished I was back in Paris, but I also wished for the fighting to go on in Italy. I wished for Italy to be punished just like I was being punished. I knew it was wrong and that it was mean, but I wished it anyway.

Rome

In late April of that year, 1849, it appeared that summer was coming early. The sun shone bright and the days were warm, some even hot. Mother was, as ever, busy with her work at the hospitals, but I did finally get to escape Rome. We did not go far—I, my governess, and friends of my mother Mr. and Mrs. Mancini and their two daughters, Biancha and Chiara, who were a few years older than me.

We took a trip to Lardo di Nemi, some thirty kilometers south of Rome, with the intention of spending a few days swimming and hiking and enjoying the early arrival of summer.

On our second day at Largo di Nemi, our holiday was cut short and we were made to hurry back to Rome.

"What's happened, Mother?" said Chiara, the elder of the two girls.

"Rome has been attacked," she said.

Biancha asked the exact question that was on my mind: "Then why are we going back there?"

"We'll be safe there," Mrs. Mancini said then she looked at me. "We're going to the hospital to see your mother."

"Is she all right?" I asked. Despite the animosity and anger I'd been feeling towards her, I loved my mother. When Mrs. Mancini announced that we were rushing back to Rome to see my mother, I was genuinely concerned and afraid.

"She's fine," said Mrs. Mancini. "But we're going to have to bunker down, and your mother will be able to keep us safe." She looked at her daughters. "Everything's going to be all right. Don't worry."

As the carriage raced toward Rome, the rapid clip-clop of the horses hooves mimicked the excited beating of my heart. I was definitely worried. And judging by the expressions on the others' faces, I was not the only one.

When we arrived at the hospital, we set out to find my mother, which was no easy feat. People were running every which way, some wounded, leaving trails of blood behind them, while others carried those too wounded to walk on their own. I saw a young boy, probably not much older than I was. His leg had been torn or blown off above the knee. He was being carried by a man I presumed was his father who was shouting and running in circles looking for someone to help his child. The boy's face was ashen and devoid of expression. I can still see it vividly to this day.

There were other men, carrying other boys, and men carrying other men, all with limbs missing, clothes bloodied and shredded. My governess tried to shield my eyes from the horrors, but that was impossible; the horrors were all around us. And even if she had been able to shield my eyes from them, she could not have also plugged my ears, for all around us came panicked and pained cries for help while cannon fire echoed in the distance.

We did not find my mother, but a nurse who worked closely with her did find us. She assured me my mother was OK. She led us underground to a storage cellar crammed with frightened people very much like us.

"Your mother is all right, Maria," she said. "And she will come for you later, maybe in a day or two. But right now, she needs to stay in the hospital to help. You understand, don't you?"

I swallowed the lump in my throat, and I nodded. 'Is this what I have been wishing for?' I thought. 'More of this?'

I sat against a cold rock wall next to Biancha and an older woman I did not know. Bits of conversations bounced around me, too chaotic for me to piece together: names I didn't recognize; regions I had only a vague notion of; the Pope; and the French.

I broke my silence at the mention of the French,

turning to the old man who had spoken it. "Sir, did you say the French have come?"

"I'm Catholic," he said angrily. "And if Louis Napoleon III thinks that by bombing my city he's going to win my favor, he is sorely mistaken. He may be Napoleon Bonaparte's nephew, but that doesn't frighten me."

I had many questions but no chance to ask them. Another man joined in the conversation. "We may be Catholics, but we're Italian, too. He didn't count on that."

"Take over the city," chimed in a third man, "and give it back to the Pope, then all of Italy's Catholics will rejoice. Ha! That's the problem with the French: they are simple-minded. All Catholics will be grateful the Pope is back in Rome, despite our brothers and sisters killed in our streets. What an idiot."

"I don't understand," I said. I turned to the old man and implored him with my questioning eyes. "You mean this bombardment—"

"We thought the Austrians were bad," he interrupted.

"The French gave us a revolutionary spirit," said the other man.

The cellar walls shook. From cannon fire or worse, I could not know.

"Here's your French revolution," said the first man, "coming right down on our heads."

I buried my face in my hands.

Biancha put her arm around me. "It's going to be all right."

I shook my head. "It's all my fault."

"What?" she asked.

"It's all my fault," I repeated over and over.

"Maria, what are you saying? This is not your fault," said Biancha. But she could not know the anger I'd been harboring in my heart. She could not fathom the wishes I'd made late at night for the French to come and rescue me, get me out of this place and take me back to France.

"I'm sorry," I said, and I wept.

"It's not your fault, Maria."

"I didn't mean it. I didn't mean it."

"Shh, it's going to be all right," said Biancha softly.

"I take it back," I uttered. "I didn't mean it. I take it back." I wiped my tears, threw my head back and shouted loud enough for whatever deity was listening to me from heaven, "I didn't mean it. I take it back!"

5

CRISTINA, 1849-1854

Rome

$\mathcal{I}$ was not going to suffer the same fate as my step-father. When the Austrians retook control of the Papal States, I did not plan to stay and wait for them to come round me up. I began planning my second exile. 'Perhaps, I will go to London,' I thought. I had a dear friend I knew could receive us and help me make arrangements. I secluded myself in the writing room and began penning my friend a letter.

I had only just finished the proper introductory saluta-tions when Mary Anne Parker knocked on the door. Mary Anne, having lost her husband in the war and now finding herself homeless, agreed to stay with me in my employ-ment as nurse for both me and Maria.

"Yes, enter," I said.

"Cristina, there is a man, Father Moricami, here to see you."

The name was familiar to me, yet I could not place it

exactly. However, it did bring a positive sensation so it was with a happy spirit that I went to greet him.

Upon seeing his face, I was immediately reminded of our last encounter. Father Moricami had been faithful to the Pope and had harbored a few of the Pope's soldiers, nursing them back to health in his home. When he was found out, he was taken by Garibaldi's men who did not know what to do with him. They feared imprisoning a priest would have more negative consequences than letting him free to offer support to the enemy.

It had been in the papacy's best interest to keep our Italian nations separated, and so they had lent their support to the Austrians, an unfortunate turn for us. One has to wonder what could have been different if they had instead supported the Italians, rather than doing their best to divide us.

The wounded soldiers from the Pope's army were brought to my hospital and they told me of the father's fate. I did not want to keep the Pope's soldiers in our hospital, yet they still needed time and care to recover. I suggested to Garibaldi's men that we return the wounded soldiers to the care of Father Moricami and that he not be captured. "It is not the wounded nor is it the empathetic who are our enemy."

I intervened on his behalf, not out of any respect for his vocation or even sympathy for his plight, but rather for practical motives. Nevertheless, Father Moricami thanked me. And now that my people had been vanquished by his, he stood at my door and requested entry.

I invited him into the sitting room and asked Mary Anne if she wouldn't mind putting the kettle on.

"That is very kind, Princess Trivulzo, but I will not be staying long."

"Oh?" His tone and his demeanour forewarned that he had somber news to deliver.

"Your address is not a mystery to the Austrians, neither is your fervent support of the rebellion."

"I'm not surprised," I said.

"Then you know that you cannot stay."

I looked away from him. What he said was true, but I didn't like hearing it, especially not from him: someone who would undoubtedly benefit from the loss of my people's freedom, someone who would flourish under the restored occupation.

"Do you have somewhere to go?" he asked sheepishly.

I snapped my head and fixed him sternly. "Of course I have somewhere to go, if that is what I choose."

He slouched even further in his seat. It was apparent he was trying to make himself small and had not intended to turn the knife in my freshly made wound. "I apologize for my bluntness."

"There's no need."

"But you must know that they've set up checkpoints at all the exits of the city. They are catching all those who attempt to flee."

I was not surprised by this news, though a bit surprised by the source from which I was receiving it. "Did you come here tonight to divulge military secrets?"

He smirked. "It is like you said, do you remember? 'Our fight is not with those who express empathy.'"

I straightened in my chair and smoothed out my skirts. "I'm afraid, father, you are mistaken. What I did for you was out of practical necessity, not an expression of empathy or compassion."

He chuckled. "Even if I believed you—"

"Why wouldn't you?"

He put his hands in the air, open palms out. "Very well. Consider what I am doing then as an act of practical necessity, for my own good, and not an act of empathy. For I could not sleep at night if I knew some harm fell upon you and I did not act to prevent it."

I paused a moment and weighed his words. "And what is this act of practical necessity you intend to carry out?"

He took in a deep breath. And as he prepared himself to answer, Mary Anne entered with the tea. He seemed relieved for the intrusion. Though she looked at him with a suspicious eye, he responded with a warm smile and offered her his sincere thanks. I accepted a cup of tea as well, for the form, but I did not touch it.

"Will you need anything else, Cristina?" Mary Anne asked me.

"No, thank you, Mary Anne. I will be seeing Father Moricami out shortly."

She nodded, glanced again furtively at my guest then left us.

Father Moricami took a sip of his tea then, finding it too hot, set the cup back on its saucer. He wiped his mouth then cleared his throat. "I have a carriage," he said, and for the first time that night he looked me straight in the eyes and he spoke with a serious tone, stripped of the polite formalities of earlier. "The carriage won't be stopped. And I have people setting sail from Salerno to Malta. You would be granted safe passage, I assure you."

"Malta," I said, though not to him but rather just to hear the name from my own lips. "I could consider going to Malta."

"I'm afraid you must consider it," he said with urgency. "And I'm afraid you must agree to let me help you."

"I must?"

He nodded. "Soldiers, I've heard, plan to come for you in the morning. You mustn't be here when they arrive."

Though his words did shock me, I remained stoic and did not blink. "How can you be sure?"

"I could be mistaken, of course. But I don't think that I am. The orders have been given, and I am close with the brother of one of the soldiers tasked to carry them out. That is how I came to hear of the operation. I've also been led to believe that your standing will not grant you any clemency, quite the opposite, no doubt."

"No doubt," I repeated to myself.

"The only question that remains is: when they do come, will they find anyone here, or will you be safely on your way to Malta?"

Of course he was being kind to warn me. He was quite possibly saving me from imprisonment or worse. Yet, despite this fact, I wanted him out of my home. He may have come as a friend, but he was still telling me I needed to leave: leave my home, leave my country. I had known this day was coming, and soon. But I wanted to leave on my own terms, in my own time, and to my own chosen destination.

"I took the liberty of requesting the carriage come for

you tonight," he said. "Should you choose to accept my offer."

"How can I not?"

He smiled meekly and cast his eyes down to the floor. "I'm glad to hear you say that."

"Of course, I am not travelling alone," I said, as if I could still dictate at least some demands. "My child will come with me, Maria. She is twelve years old. And Mary Anne, I will not abandon her."

"Of course," he said. "That is perfectly natural. That will be fine."

I stood abruptly. "Well, then, I must prepare. I have to pack, don't I?"

He stood as well. "You'll have to pack, lightly, I'm afraid."

I walked him to the door.

"It was good to see you again, Princess Trivulzo."

I did not respond, but rather stood holding the door open for him.

"I wish sincerely that it had been under different circumstances," he continued.

"So do I," I said.

"Take care of yourself, Princess Trivulzo. Adieu."

Rome

Maria, Mary Anne and I loaded a trunk each into the carriage. We got in; the driver shut the door and we were off. With not even the time to look back over the shoulder and lament a forced goodbye; not even the chance to touch the walls fondly and reflect on all the memories you would keep. Our home in Rome was gone to us, already relegated to a past too foreign to us to miss.

"Everything's going to be all right," I said to Maria. She looked more tired than afraid. "Do you want to take a nap during the ride? We'll be on the coast in four hours. Then you can sleep on the boat, if you'd like or you can look out and watch the sea."

She came and sat with me, in my arms, and rested her head on my bosom.

"I'm sorry I did all this," she murmured.

"What? You didn't do any of this, my dear. None of this is your fault."

"I wished for us to leave," she said.

I kissed her on the head. "It's all right, dear."

We arrived on the coast in the dead of night and were quickly whisked onto a small ferry. Again, we were afforded no time to turn from the water and look back lovingly at the land we'd regret, no time to offer a final eulogia and make eloquent promises of an eventual return. We boarded our vessel, where already a family of five from Hungary and two young couples from Italy waited to be exiled. We were soon joined by another family of three from Poland, then we set sail. Our cabin was cramped and offered no view I had promised Maria she could have of the sea.

"Do you want to go on deck and look at the sea?" I asked her.

She shook her head no and laid her sleepy body down on my lap.

Had we gone on deck, we would have had but a short moment to watch the sea. Our passage was troubled with high winds and rough waters. Our vessel rose and lunged and rocked and jerked.

'Poor Maria,' I thought. But she slept, more or less, soundly through our passage. While I battled with nausea to keep from getting sick or passing out or both.

We arrived in Malta, a pitiful cargo.

~

Malta

I did not give Malta a chance. Perhaps the island had its charms, but as it was a destination imposed on me, I could never let myself become susceptible to them. I longed for my green gardens, my enchanting lakes of Lombardy. I had neither: the familiarity of living in a country very close to what I didn't want to leave nor transported to a place whose originality gripped the attention. Resemblance sweetens the regrets and diversity stuns them. But in Malta all is pale and dull, in a word, nostalgic.

My poor child, Maria, her spirits were never high during those months in Malta.

"Do you miss Rome?" I asked her.

"No, I never liked Rome," she said.

"Do you miss Paris?" I asked.

She put a finger to her chin, pursed her lips and looked up at the sky. "Hmm, do I miss Paris?" After a moment of reflection she pulled her finger from her chin, dropped her head and said, "I used to like Paris. But I don't like Paris anymore. And I don't miss it."

"So, where should we go, then? Milan?"

She furrowed her brow in confusion. "Are we allowed back in Italy?"

I ran my hand over her head, straightening her hair. "Maybe not right now, but in a few months, possibly." She seemed surprised. "I'm writing letters." I smiled at her. "Your mother knows a lot of people."

In Italy the Pope had returned to Rome, the Austrians had returned to power, and a few exiles were allowed to return. It was a delicate maneuver the Austrians attempted, trying to find a balance between letting back enough exiles to not further instigate another revolt and punishing enough of them to not admit another revolt.

Though my support for the republic was well known and could not be overstated, so was my support for those few who whether soldier or politician, writer or bureaucrat were accorded grace and allowed to reintegrate society.

I wrote to them to prepare for an eventual return to Italy.

The responses were slow to arrive and when they did, they brought no relief or hope of relief but rather anger and despair.

I sat at my writing desk contemplating my next letter while simultaneously trying to muster up the resolve to actually pen it. Mary Anne knocked on the door.

"Yes, enter." I was relieved to see a friendly face. "You have perfect timing," I said.

She held a letter in her hand and waved it for me to

see. "Let's hope the news I've brought is as perfect as my timing."

I held out my hand, and she gave me the letter. "Please, won't you sit and keep me company?"

"Gladly," she said. "Are you going to read the letter? It's from General Radetzky."

I did not share the same enthusiasm for the letter as she showed. General Radetzky had already sent word saying he was in no position to help. "I'll read the letter," I said. "But prepare yourself for disappointment."

"Why do you say that?"

I opened the envelope with a sigh and unfolded the missive. "They write either to ask me for money or to condemn me for my ideas and say they can have nothing more to do with me."

"Really?"

I looked across at her from under the letter. "Yes, really. Sometimes they manage to do both in the same message."

"That's a shame," she said.

The letter I was currently reading was no exception. I finished it and put it in the drawer with the others.

"But surely General Radetzky—"

I shook my head.

The expression on her face went from sadness to indignation. I had already passed through those stages, but I'd been keeping the details of my efforts at returning to Italy quiet. I didn't want to give her or Maria cause for further distress.

"But you supplied nearly half his army," she said.

I nodded. "And now he disowns me."

Mary Anne straightened her shawl with a huff and a tug. I found her offense endearing. I had company in my affliction.

"A man with dangerous ideas, he can be reasoned with or killed. But a woman can only be suffered."

She gasped and turned to me with an appalled look on her face.

I pointed down to the letter on my desk. "His words. Not mine."

"After all you've done for him," she uttered with indignation.

"A man who fires on a soldier and grievously wounds him is more welcome back than the woman who nurses him and tends to his wounds," I said. "Violence and aggression, the kings and the popes can contend with violence and aggression. But empathy, that terrifies them."

We sat a moment in silence until Mary Anne turned to me and said, "Does this mean we won't be returning to Italy?"

"Why would we want to?" I stood and walked from my desk over to her. In doing so, I caught sight of the door, which had been left half open. Beyond the threshold, in the other room, I saw Maria, standing in the corner, facing me.

"Maria," I called out.

She turned and ran.

I ran after her, down the corridor toward her bedroom. "Maria."

She had not shut the door behind her, but I knocked quietly as I stepped softly inside. Maria was in her bed

with her arms wrapped around her legs and her knees up
to her chin.

"Maria, is everything all right?" I approached her and
motioned to the side of the bed. "May I sit?"

She nodded. "I'm sorry I was overhearing. I only
wanted to come tell you something."

"That's all right, dear. What is it you wanted to
tell me?"

She bit down on the inside of her cheek and glanced
to the wall on her right. "I can't remember." She looked
back at me. "It probably wasn't anything important."

I smiled and touched her arm. "That's all right, dear.
Did you hear what I and Mary Anne were saying?"

Again, she nodded.

"And how does that make you feel?"

She shrugged. "I didn't want to go back to Italy
anyway, you know?"

I nodded and brushed the fringe from her cheeks.
"Don't worry, dear. We're going to go somewhere nice,
somewhere beautiful, somewhere fun."

"Where there is no fighting?" she asked.

This time it was I who glanced over at the wall. The
notion of living somewhere where there was no fighting
passed my mind. It was a pleasant notion, for a second
then it became quite a frightening notion. 'Not to fight
would be not to live,' I thought and I shuddered.

I looked back at Maria and offered her a soft smile.
"There will still be fighting, and thankfully so. But we'll
fight another way."

～

Turkey

Dear Caroline,

I write to you today with some distressing news: it has come to my attention that the safety of myself and my family will be compromised if I was to remain in Italy. I was visited by a man who carried this news to me, and I made arrangements to leave this country as soon as I could.

It saddens me to know that I will have to set aside my political passions for the moment and retreat much like a cowardly rat, but I have a child to consider. Though I'm still young, and though I can still make the changes I wish to in this world, I have to consider how Maria may fare in a hostile environment.

I wish that I could disclose our destination or our source of information to you, but discretion has always been a friend of mine, and I cannot make the mistake of risking everything at the moment.

Once I have reached our new temporary home, I will write again, updating you on our wellbeing and our progress.

Sincerely,
Cristina

I had to change the course of my ideas and break with politics at the moment. But, at the same time, I had to keep fighting for what I believed in; to give up fighting, for me, would be to cease being. I was too young and still breathed the air of my youth and with it all of its ideals and wonders. I wanted to live in a land full of breath-taking sights and baffling contrasts and contradictions. Without them, I would be constantly pining for Italy, which I refused to do. Living on regrets is repulsive to my nature.

I confided in Mary Anne, who more and more was providing me with much needed comfort and solace. She was wise and caring, and there was never an idea or a thought that wasn't made clearer and grander by first sharing it with her. We took a late evening tea on the terrace.

"If I have to give up the realization of my wishes in Italy," I said to her, "Then I want to embrace a kind of life that provides me with sources of interest."

"You have no lack of interests, Cristina."

"That is true. But these interests that will comprise my new life must erase the memory of the old one, or at least of what stings the most."

"You still have too much force and too much vitality to talk about leaving your old life," she said.

"But it's being erased whether I want it to or not. Until our youth lasts, our life is comparable to those plants that draw from the air their food and have no supports: you can then transplant them. Later we grow the roots and from these we draw livelihood. Exile then becomes lethal."

"An uprooted plant," said Mary Anne, "when it is replanted, does it not flourish?"

"Possibly. I have not yet reached that point, I have no strong habits and my feelings are not yet clinging to the ground."

"The air, the subtle and spiritual element of the thought, is enough for me," she said.

"How long will I be like that?" She did not respond. How could she? "I do not know, myself," I added. "But to choose a final residence in a fertile land in the center of a lovely landscape." I sighed and looked up longingly at the ceiling. "I will wait until the hour when my strengths will abandon me and I will not be able to go on looking. First, I want to travel."

"Traveling would do us good," she said.

"What would you say if we went to Constantinople?"

"Constantinople?" She seemed as surprised to hear the name as I'd been surprised to be speaking it. "Why Constantinople?"

"It has a rich history, proud people, and famous encounters," I said, convincing myself more and more as I spoke. "The entrance is not prohibited by any political party."

"Constantinople," she repeated.

"Perhaps not Constantinople, exactly," I continued, "but somewhere in Turkey. Perhaps, all of Turkey. We could travel. We don't lack in possabilities."

She did not ask me to elaborate, and thankfully so, for

I doubt I would have been able to. The truth was that once I had renounced the habits and ambitions of my former life, all else became possible. Yet, without the singular focus of working towards a free and unified Italy, I had little idea of where the possibilities would take me. Furthermore, there was the practical side of my present reality: the Austrians had seized my resources, we were not wanted in Italy, and I had a twelve-year-old daughter to consider. The only travel we would do for the time being was travel to our next destination, where hopefully I could give Maria some semblance of stability and I could find a worthy cause to dedicate myself to.

Turkey was the dream my present limitations inspired. I secured credit and bought a farm outside of Anatolia, in Çakmakoğlu. I had never envisioned such a rural setting to make my home. From Milan to Paris to Rome, big cities, salons and soirees, to a small farm in Çakmakoğlu, it was precisely the kind of change I needed at the time. I wanted to part ways with the past and embrace new possibilities for the future, and appropriately, first I would need to embrace new people from a new culture and embrace a very different way of life.

Turkey

Our time in Çakmakoğlu was indeed as solitary as I had hoped. Mary Anne remained as dedicated to the education of Maria as I hoped she would, and I was happy to watch

Maria bloom. Çakmakoğlu, it seemed, suited her more than the salon of Paris and our home in Milan.

While Maria studied, I toiled away working to provide for our small family in a way that had previously been unknown to me. In the beginning it was easy for me to get lost in tending the land, I imagined the dirt around my nails as a badge of honor to bear proudly.

Yet, I'd never been a woman who could rest easy without having some greater purpose driving me. I watched as Maria grew in much the same way the plants around me, but I grew restless and suffered from ennui.

My brief escapes from life of solitude was the trips to the market into Ankara itself. Usually I travelled by myself, preferring to have the time away from Maria and Mary Anne. I also enjoyed the occasional social event with one dignitary or another.

There were many refugees who had fled to Turkey following the failure of the coup to which I had dedicated my life. I enjoyed meeting up with my fellow Italians, forging new friendships and alliances.

I also met several Hungarians, who themselves were refugees of a war that struck near and dear to my heart, though I did try to avoid spending too much time with them, lest I be assumed to be an associate. Many of the refugees of the war of independence in Hungary were being asked to convert to Islam in order to avoid extradition, something that I had no wish to be a part of.

As a stolid Catholic, like many in my country, I found Islam to be unconventional to say the least. That is to say while the very strictures and heart of the religion were similar to Christianity and Catholicism, their behaviour and customs were nothing but sinful.

During one of my forays into Ankara I was encouraged by some new acquaintances to visit a hammam. I was told that it was the height of luxury and an experience to look forward to.

Curious, I decided that I would accompany my new friend to this bath house to see for myself whether it was everything that I was told it would be.

I have to say, I've never been more unsettled than I was upon my visit. No matter where one looked, the eyes landed on naked flesh, such that I felt the need close my eyes as soon as I entered. To my chagrin, my friend found my ill ease to be amusing and antiquated, which she freely spoke of to whomever chose to make my acquaintance.

It was told the unclad form, the expanse of female anatomy, and exposure to the very nature we were born to, was a holy experience. My friend, who had spent more of her life in Ankara than I ever did, was at ease with the licentious atmosphere, and indeed basked in it.

My haste of departure from the hammam remained a point of contention between us, one that we were never able to fully overcome. During my time at home on the farm, I wrote several essays outlining my detailed thoughts of my participation in such an archaic ritual.

These women believed they were promoting a sisterhood of acceptance, to which I strongly disagreed. The rights of women had long since been reduced to our basest form, our sexuality, and if we are to move forward as a sex, we needed to rise above it.

The harems were even worse, and though my friend

shared lewd details with me in the hopes of encouraging me to appreciate it, I avoided it much like I did those who may wish to convert me to Islam.

In many ways I was thankful that I didn't bring Maria with me on those outings. Young women tended to be impressionable and delicate in those matters; I quite feared it would have upset her more than me to participate in the culture of hammams and harems.

My dearest Caroline,

> *It seems beyond my abilities to describe some of the things that I have been witness to since my arrival in Çakmakoğlu; I'm quite thankful that many of my trips into the more urbanized areas of the country have been on my own, otherwise I fear my dear Maria would have had an education she's not yet ready to receive.*

> *I have heard of harems and hammams, of course, generally, though, not through a source who was able to give a first hand account of the experiences; my understanding is that men are not welcome into such establishments and therefore it would be difficult for them to describe. However, I had the luck of meeting a woman, a Lady Catherine Belmont, who is also an immigrant to*

the area, and I must admit, she has had
far more time to become acclimated to
the culture here than I ever plan to.

Ms. Belmont and I would communicate
through letters occasionally, but usually I
called upon her when I visited the city. I
have to say that while I found the
countryside to be a peaceful respite, it
sometimes failed to inspire contentment
within me, hence my trips into the city
which exposed me to humanity and the
souls of people again.

During my last foray into the city, I met Ms.
Belmont at a small cafe where we enjoyed
Türk kahvesi, Turkish Coffee, which is
comprised of finely ground beans that are
filtered. It's not unlike the coffee we have
in Italy, it is richer, darker and leaves no
bitter aftertaste on the tongue. My
understanding is that it is also more
potent than what we are used to, and
thus we are served in small cups, making
the drink seemingly delicate.

After our drinks, Ms. Belmont invited me to
go with her to participate in a local
custom, which was the use of the
hammam. I have to say I'm not naive,
nor am I unread, so I didn't enter this

*situation without the knowledge that I
may be uncomfortable, but curiosity did
get the better of me and I attended the
hammam with her.*

*Caroline, it was distressing to see the state
that these women allowed themselves to
lounge in; not a stitch of clothing to be
had on any of them, and they all acted as
though their nakedness, their lascivious
behaviour were the most natural thing in
the world. I hardly knew where to rest
my eyes and found my distress to be quite
alarming, though Ms. Belmont seemed to
find humour in it.*

*I have to wonder what kind of culture
encourages such behaviour from their
women? How are they to raise themselves
to be seen beyond their base sexuality if
they regard it as part of their culture? It
was unbelievably degrading just for me to
set my eyes upon them, imagine if a man
were to be present, though I'm told that
isn't permitted. Still, it is a practice that I
am shocked is still taking place in this
day and age, one that makes women seem
more like chattel than humans worthy of
dignity.*

I had considered bringing Maria in with me

that day, and I'm ever so grateful that I
changed my mind on the matter. This
experience was horrifying for me, a full
grown woman who has seen and
participated in acts of intimacy, I cannot
imagine how Maria would have felt.

In any case, I assure you Ms. Belmont and I
will not be conversing as regularly in the
future. The fact that she found humour
in my obvious discomfort suggests that she
may feel so inclined to bring me into
similar situations, and that is something
that I will be avoiding.

I look forward to hearing your thoughts on
my experience, perhaps you can help me
to view the matter in a way that leaves
me feeling less disturbed.

Sincerely,
Cristina

After some time on the farm I began to feel a wanderlust
that couldn't be shaken. Even my treks into Ankara did
little to settle my soul, and I found myself daydreaming
like a maiden over maps of Turkey.

It was on one such occasion that I decided that Maria
and I should make a pilgrimage to Jerusalem. In my mind,
there is no holier place than that where our saviour was

born. Besides, Maria had yet to be baptized, and I have to admit I was quite entranced with the romanticism of the idea of my daughter being christened there.

Maria, of course, balked at my suggestion, as she has always suffered from the wont to do the exact opposite of anything I wish. However, I firmly reminded her that as she was not yet an adult, she was in my care and must travel with me wherever I went. To my relief, Mary Anne encouraged Maria to respect her mother and her mother's wishes, and we left our home in Çakmakoğlu to see Maria properly adopted into Christianity.

Though it pained me to travel further away from my native country, I did find myself quite ebulant about our journey. I felt that Maria would benefit greatly from a spiritual journey such as the one we had embarked upon.

While on our journey, I had left the farm in the hands of a man from Alsace. I didn't want the place to wither in our absence, but I also felt the pull of new horizons deep in my soul. We needed a home, our little safe haven of nature and wonder, to return to.

Though I longed for Italy, I knew that I could not yet return to her soil. The political landscape had not settled enough to permit someone of my persuasion to once again become a member of the Italian community.

We passed through many towns on our journey to the holy land. Some were more sophisticated than others, while some proved to be primitive, their homes made of wood and mud and falling to ruin. These sights humbled me, while further enforcing the desire in me to make some kind of prominent change in our world.

That places like these could be left for people to live in

while others lived in untold wealth and luxury, with never a want in their little lives.

I believe these sights had a similar effect on Maria, though at her age, she was turning inward and less likely to share her assessments of the culture with me. I think in some ways she resented me for exposing her to such horrid scenes, but as a liberalist, I felt that an education in the poverty of some nations was essential so that she may have a worldly view as she formed her opinions.

Upon reaching the city of Angora, we experienced a setback in our journey that irritated me. Due to some error on my passport, a minor thing that should have been over-looked as far as I was concerned, we were forced to remain in the city for a fortnight—the kaymakam requested a payment of $600 with an avarice that astounded me, and I was forced to write out a cheque for the amount; it was a demand that I would have my bank in Istanbul forestall.

The expense of such an undertaking was one I was frightened to contemplate. Yet there I was with my daughter and her governess and we needed a place to lay down our bodies and rest on occasion. Not to mention the need for sustenance for ourselves and our animals, but I was confident that my cleverness would secure us.

I was correct in that assumption, and relieved too, as I met a colleague of someone I'd known in Ankara. This Tcherkess suffered from a painful ailment in his eye and I applied my experience as a nurse with astute care, thus relieving him of the torment he'd been dealing with.

To my delight, the Tcherkess offered to help us in our time of need, and offered us a place to settle while we waited for diplomatic matters to be sorted. Though I must admit I first felt reluctance when I saw the place he would have us call our home.

Dervishes were something I'd heard about in my former life, like a mystical being that only existed in the minds of men, much like a unicorn or leprechaun. Never did I expect to have the pleasure of making the acquaintance of one such a man, let alone a convent.

"This is where we will be staying?" asked Maria when we first arrived. I could see that she was immediately enchanted by the idea of these individuals.

"Yes, these dervishes have graciously offered to host us while we wait on the kaymakam."

Mary Anne remained quiet and I had the sense that unlike Maria, she understood the molestation our nerves would have to endure, much like I did. Still, she supported my decision, ushering Maria into the place without voicing any grievances.

The building was more than modest, as were our rooms, but I appreciated that we would not be exposed to the elements while we waited, nor would we go hungry. The furniture was sparse, indeed practically non-existent as these dervishes declined the accoutrements that we three were accustomed to.

To be clear, I held no resentment for the dervishes, in that regard; in fact I admired their dedication and tenacity for this. A life without the distraction of physical belongings wasn't something to admonish, rather it held a simplicity that was perhaps admirable.

No, for me, the issue lay not in their beliefs, but rather

their religious ceremonies that often included strange dances and sometimes harming oneself.

Outside of the convent, dervishes were highwaymen, imposters and idlers as far as I was concerned. I held hope that the convent would help to tame their savagery and make them hospitable.

I was invited to observe one of their practices and I have to say that I was as disturbed by their action as much I had been at the hammam. Instead of seeing expanses of unmarked flesh, I was instead seeing flesh that had webs of scars on it; as a way of seeking commune with their deity, these zealots were cutting into their own skin.

Just when I thought I had reached the limits of the insanity of such nonsense, another man would approach the injured man and purport to heal the first's injury with his saliva. I can say with honesty that the spectacle I had naively agreed to witness did leave it's own scars in my mind.

The majority of our time in the convent was spent in isolation or wandering the streets of the city. Mary Anne and Maria continued on with my daughter's education, of course, and I occupied my mind with writing essays which I would send off to different newspapers in the hopes of publication.

Dear Caroline,

> *I hope this missive finds you well and in good
> spirits, I'm writing to you from Ankara
> where I've had the delight of making the*

acquaintance of several dervishes; yes, of that persuasion.

However, these particular men are not found on the road, they have in fact gathered in a convent here in the city and have offered Maria, myself and our party a place to rest for the time being. As such, I've been witness to some of their more queer and unconventional practices, and I have to admit that it all seems like a bit of nonsense to me.

Thankfully, the sight of them dancing doesn't make me as discomforted as the hammam that I have previously written about, but there are practices that I definitely do not approve of, and indeed have caused me some uneasiness.

Their rituals, though central to their beliefs, seem heretic to me and wildly inappropriate; it's as though the dance itself summons a madness in each man, one that can only be quenched with their own pain.

I have watched these men during their religious rights, and the sights I have seen are indeed macabre; these men would flagellate themselves, cut themselves and

dance until blisters broke on their feet.
Then, just when you were certain you'd
seen the darkest side of the ceremony, they
would take it one step farther causing a
deep disturbance that I don't feel I shall
ever fully escape.

As each man was injured, another would
come along and lick the wounds of the
injured. It was explained to me, in rather
gruesome detail, that the saliva from the
dervishes could heal any wound, and
thus they would behave like wounded
animals.

My pallor must have been off, for my host
was quick to bring me back to my room,
where I spent the evening in
contemplative silence. I shared nothing of
this experience with Maria or Mary
Anne, who was already discomforted by
the choice I'd made to remain at the
convent.

I had been aware that the dervishes were
considered uncivilized at best, but the
extent of it had been beyond my
knowledge. Seeing such displays makes
me long for my home and the stability
and security that Maria and I had
known there.

*I have penned an essay that shall be
published in several newspapers in Italy
as well as in François's paper. I'm sure
these insights will startle many, and
perhaps lead some to the belief that I
have exaggerated; rest assured, I have not.*

*We are currently en route to Jerusalem, where
I plan to have Maria christened; it's
perhaps a romantic notion to wish my
daughter be baptized in the place of Jesus'
birth, but since when have I let
something as silly as that stand in the
way of a grand adventure?*

*I have brought with me a small group of
men, Maria and our governess Ms.
Parker. Maria is still receiving her
education on this journey, as it will not
be of a short duration, but I feel the
experience is teaching her far more than
any books could.*

*I know that I'm eagerly anticipating all of the
different discoveries along the way,
though I'm hoping none are as dreadful
as that of the dervishes or the hammam.*

*During my time, I am not only writing to
you, my dear friend, but I am also
writing essays that I hope to have*

> *published in newspapers or perhaps in a*
> *book. I feel the world needs to learn more*
> *about the Ottoman Empire and their*
> *dangerously uncivilized ways.*
>
> *For the time being, we are comfortable and I*
> *will write to you as soon as the next*
> *opportunity arises.*

Sincerely,
Cristina

I have to admit that I had not given appropriate consideration to the mountain passes that we three had to trek
through, but I'm glad to say that we persevered, though
we were often fatigued once we made our way through.

The remainder of our journey was fraught with many
dangerous trips through mountain passes, but along the
way we were able to make several acquaintances who were
able to see us through to our final destination safely.

All in all the journey toward Jerusalem was as educational for me as it was my daughter. The sights we encoun-
tered and the inhabitants of each region welcomed us and
helped us along our journey. In a way it would be
romantic to imagine they all played a part in Maria's christening, but I fear I'm too logical to entertain that notion
for any length of time.

At one point we visited Alexandretta, but I'm afraid to
say the place was inhospitable and I made haste to move
the three of us out of there as quickly as we could; though

I have to admit the bay was magnificent and would have been reason enough to stay. Still, I had my daughter to think of and I couldn't risk her simply for a lovely view.

I enjoyed Antioch, it was a welcoming city that I, Mary Anne and Maria all enjoyed. However, it was not our final destination and so we were forced to leave for the holy land in order to arrive in a timely manner for Maria's christening.

The next set of mountain passes were not just foreboding in their physical presence and stature, they were also inhabited by cells of fighting soldiers. Thus the journey had another layer of jeopardy and instability for us to consider.

Though I felt my hand was forced, I did commission some soldiers, nothing more than a ragtag group of mercenaries, unfortunately, to safeguard us as we crossed the border. I cannot say that I felt completely secure, but I had taken the best of my options and fate had left me no other choice. I worried that it would stress Maria and Marry Anne, I cannot imagine being around such crass men at such an impressionable age.

Thankfully, we made our way into Syria with no incident worse than a dueling of words that I found to be somewhat entertaining, though Maria and Mary Anne did not agree with me on that point.

The landscape in Syria was breathtaking to say the least. I was left struck with a feeling of awe as we travelled through. It was truly one of the most beautiful places I'd seen since leaving my home country. I did my best to describe, but I'm certain my words were unable to convey the true beauty that I saw.

· · ·

Dear Caroline,

> *We have arrived in Syria, and it is a breathtaking sight indeed. I fear that my description of the beauty cannot do it justice, and so I shall not attempt it here, though I hope one day you are able to see this.*

> *Our journey thus far has not been one that I anticipated in entirety. I have come across some situations that have required a delicate hand and a silver tongue, and for that I am thankful of my experience in speaking with people of various different classes.*

> *I fear that Maria has had some reservations about my decision regarding this journey. The mountain passes have been excruciating, to say the least, and tested our endurance beyond measure. I'm thankful that Maria and I have had a fairly active lifestyle, which helped to prepare us for the trek. I fear that if we had been the type of person to enjoy lounging as a hobby we would not have had within us the will to push through.*

On the last peaks alone I was forced to
employ mercenaries to ensure our safety as
we crossed the border from Turkey into
Syria. I'm afraid the experience was not
pleasant for Maria or Mary Anne, but I
found the slurs sent in our party's
direction to be unimaginative and thus
entertaining. Of course, I could not
receive such an attack without returning
my own fire; I'm the first to admit that it
was potentially not the wisest idea for me
to partake in the conversation.

Unfortunately for us, it doesn't seem that the
mountain passes have come to an end,
there are many more for us to pass
through, but I have faith in our party
and in our stamina, and I'm certain to
write to you from Jerusalem, or perhaps
Nazareth.

I look forward to resting my eyes on those holy
lands and the purity I think it will bring
to my soul. Perhaps I shall feel like a new
person once I leave.

Sincerely,
Cristina

I found the candor and good faith of the British and

American missionaries to be far more remarkable than their tact or intelligence. The orientals were wise to their game and conversion to Christianity had become a profitable endeavor. In each community they were gifted more capital as they converted and with the capital became quite wealthy after investing it. I found it disconcerting to see wealth, commerce and religion so closely tied.

In the Galilee mountains, we came up against conditions which could not be overcome with a banknote. As I had mentioned, the mountainous passes proved to be titans of such elemental monstrosity that we were often beleaguered by mother nature's own forces.

We were a party of five travelling through the mountains, on our way to Nazareth. There was myself, Maria, Mary Anne, along with a guide and a servant to help with bringing our things. Altogether there were six horses, one for each of us ladies, one each for the servant, our guide, and one packhorse to carry my desk and some of Maria's educational tools.

Up until this point in our journey we had all been blessed with good health with the exception of a minor malady that is common for anyone. We were well into the wilderness before we first noticed one of the horses drooping its head and starting to lag.

Upon my suggestion, the guide agreed that we should perhaps stop to give the horses time to catch their breath, as the mountainous region proved to be more strenuous than we'd first hoped. Indeed, making our way leading the horses was a difficult process and in the end, we ladies had resorted to tying our dresses above our knees so that we did not trip as we maneuvered our way through.

"My lady," said my guide, Achmed, with a worried look on his face. "I'm afraid we are not going to make our way through before night arrives, and it will be difficult to keep our footing after the sun goes down."

"You want us to stay in the mountains?" chirped Maria from behind me, Mary Anne put a hand on her arm and she blushed before apologizing for her outburst.

"It is more risky to attempt the way than to stay in the mountains?" I asked. Though I would not let my daughter know it, I was as concerned as she, and did not wish to spend our evening exposed to the elements.

"I would not advise it," he said. "Our horses are not well, the roan looks ready to faint, and some of the others are not looking well. They need fresh water and rest or they will not survive to see Nazareth."

I examined the roan myself and decided he was correct in his assumption of illness. I felt it would be foolish of us to try to proceed through the evening, risking both our own lives and that of our trusty companions.

"Very well, but we can't just sleep out in the open. The cold will settle here soon and these horses will need to be kept warm. Not to mention ourselves, we are hardly prepared for a night in the open."

"As it happens, my lady, I am familiar with this area and know of a structure that is not far from here. It's not the accommodation that you would normally experience, but it will be dry and provide some shelter."

When Achmed had told us that the structure was nearby, I had presumed we would be there shortly, but my assumption was incorrect, we did have to walk for quite some time, even going so far as to meander from the path that we were following. I discovered Achmed was true to his word, though the walk was cumbersome and hot, when we came upon a structure constructed of logs and clay.

He was correct to say that my usual accommodations were far more comfortable than what this particular domicile had to offer. However, he had not misaligned us with fancy and falsehood, so I could not in good faith be disappointed with what was before me.

The horses were quickly undressed of their saddles and their burdens. All of them were sweating heavily and while we had rationed enough water for the horses and ourselves, we gave some of our portion to the animals. It was disheartening to see such creatures in the clutches of such an illness. Achmed suggested that perhaps they had been exposed to a germ of some kind along the way, or perhaps the feed we'd purchased in Syria had turned, but either way it was clear to see they were in distress.

The roan laid down as soon as the opportunity arose, huffing as though she'd just finished a long gallop. Maria sat next to her, holding the water skin and trying to urge the animal to drink or eat, but it seemed uninterested, despite her best efforts.

"Isn't there anything we can do to ease their suffering?" she asked. I knelt beside her and rubbed the roan's neck.

"My darling, I'm afraid we don't have the resources with us to cure an illness such as this. We don't even have the expertise to declare what they are suffering from."

I saw the tears forming in her eyes before they fell, and she hugged me tight, hiding her face from the others. My

Maria was a sensitive girl and I disliked that she was exposed to such sights.

We all set up rudimentary beds for our weary bodies. Achmed and our servant, Selene, volunteered along with Mary Anne to check on the horses periodically through the night. Maria had wanted to join them, but I stood firm and advised her to get what rest she could for I knew the next day would be just as arduous, if not worse.

It was with a heavy heart that we moved on the next day whilst leaving three of our friends behind, it seemed a terrible way to die. It was unfortunate that we also were forced to leave behind some of the supplies, as well, because we were limited to three animals now.

I was happy that I had insisted upon Maria's rest, for the rest of our journey to Nazareth was on foot and it was tiresome indeed. Though the mountains were a place of natural beauty, I was grateful to once again be treading on flat ground by that afternoon. Still, with the loss of three animals, we were unfortunately unable to bring some of our stuff, specifically the tack for those horses.

I had been looking forward to seeing Nazareth, I was expecting to feel a reverence and awe induced holiness upon our arrival. Instead, we entered the city fatigued and bedraggled, each of us longing for any space where we might rest our feet.

The serendipitous meeting of Marco de Balducci, a fellow Italian and Franciscan Monk, could perhaps be considered a holy intervention. While on his way back to his convent, he saw us walking into the city and offered for us to stay with him.

"Please, I insist," he asserted, waving in the emphatic

way of my people. "You need to rest, and you will need some food."

We did not have the energy to argue with him or deny him, and in the end followed him to his convent grateful to have some place to sleep. Though the convent was bare, like many of the other places we'd been during our journey, it was far more extravagant than the shack we'd spent the night in previously.

When I looked at Nazareth in the light of day, I have to admit that I was disappointed with the city that in my mind was so hallowed. Instead, it was filled with regular people whose lives did not necessarily consist of any divine paths, but rather one of mundanity and hardship. It was rather a disappointing sight for me and I prayed that Jerusalem would live up to the ideal that I had.

"Mother," said Maria that morning, "Do you think the holy city will look like this?"

"No, darling," I said. "Jerusalem is the place where Jesus himself was born. It will be a sight that you'll not soon forget."

Marco had fed us well that night and his brothers had been considerate as well, offering a pleasant theocratic debate that I had longed for since my nights in Paris. Though the conversation was hardly political, the passion of the friendly argument was welcome.

I can't say that I look back at the city with overly fond memories, but my recollection of my time with the monks remained dear to me.

Dear Caroline,

Today we take respite in Nazareth, one of the holiest cities in all of the land and I can feel nothing but disgust as I look around me. I'm shocked at my feelings, to be honest, because we very nearly didn't make it to Nazareth to begin with.

As I've said, the mountain passes have been dangerous even in the sunniest of weather, and our most recent trek through the Galilean Mountains proved to be quite a trial.

Oftentimes we made it through the mountains tired and thirsty, but we knew that we would see the other side. This time, we weren't so certain of that. Midway through the passes our horses came down with a strange sickness, we still do not know what it was, and we were forced to spend an additional unplanned night in the mountains.

I can assure you that the thought alone was enough to fill me with terror, but I had to remain strong for Maria; she was distraught to see the horses suffering so badly and, like myself, wished there was something we could do to ease it.

Unfortunately, my skills in nursing are for humans, not animals, and I'm normally surrounded by the medicines I need, I'm not used to tending to someone without any supplies.

There was also the fact that our supplies were dwindling; we had anticipated a certain alotment of time for the pass and brought enough provisions for ourselves and the horses. An extra day and horses that were unwell meant that some of those supplies were used before they were meant to.

With deep regret, I have to say that three of our horses did not make it through the night. I wasn't sure if it was a blessing they were gone, as they were no longer in pain, or if it was a shame because the loss of life is never something to be celebrated. I know Maria was upset and I did my best to console her, but given my disposition, I'm not the most matronly person and I'm not certain how well my efforts were received.

It was a tragedy, truly, because I believe it is an experience that Maria will not soon forget, and those were not the memories I wanted her to take from this journey. I had hoped she would have a taste for adventure and spontaneity; now I fear that any spark of that has been tamped out by the shadow of ill tidings.

We made it through, though we were all weary, dehydrated, and I have to say potentially going mad with exhaustion when we finally came across a monk who offered us a place to stay. His kindness and the kindness of those in his convent were the only positive outcomes of our stay in Nazareth.

The city was destitute, muddy and ramshackle; the people walking the streets looked downtrodden and defeated by life, each lacking the spark of life or faith I had hoped to discover here. Even Maria noticed the atmosphere, and I have to say that I am concerned that Jerusalem may not be much of an improvement. I'm not sure if I can bear that, but there is only one way forward.

Sincerely,
Cristina

The final destination on our journey was on the horizon and though it had been welcomed, it had also been exhausting, so the anticipation of finally reaching the climax of our journey was urging me forward. To see my lovely girl in a white dress receiving the blessing of a priest in such a sacred place was a dream I'd been lovingly tending to for quite some time now, and I felt myself, and perhaps my soul, growing lighter as we drew nearer each day.

Unlike Nazareth, Jerusalem took my breath away. Yes, there were ordinary citizens walking the streets, much like every other metropolis I had visited, but there was an aura to this place, as though God himself was watching. It was a comforting presence that enveloped us and brought us home to the Lord himself and an experience that I will not soon forget.

Even Maria seemed awed by her surroundings; for once her haughty disposition had faded and I saw her taking in the scenery with a childlike wonder that I hadn't witnessed in years. We stayed at a local convent again, finding that those who had the least to give were often the most generous with what little they had; they were also more kind than some whose egos were inflated by their wealth.

I found a beautiful white gown for Maria at a local tailor, and the sight of her in it made my chest swell with pride such that I thought it would burst. It did not pass on me that pride, being a sin itself, was probably not something I should exhibit in such a holy land, but I felt that even God himself could not look down on this beautiful girl and not feel the same. Still, I was careful in choosing my words, but she could see it in me as I could see it in her.

I had set up a meeting with the priest of a local church

and brought Maria along with me. She seemed nervous to attend, but I could see excitement peeking out through her eyes; she had anticipated this christening as much as I, though she would never admit to such a sentimental thought.

The architecture of the church was breathtaking, leaving the sense that many holy men had spent their days there on bended knee, supplicating themselves to our Saviour. There was a heaviness to the atmosphere that left one feeling as though they were being judged as either fit for a position in the heavenly realm, or doomed to burn in the raging fires below. I was thankful that I had not deprived Maria of a religious upbringing as I had heard that other parents had done. Should she be placed on the scales of judgement, they would find her soul to be one filled with goodness, though sometimes she could be a nuisance.

As it turned out, Maria did not need to be apprehensive at all. The father questioned her on her knowledge of scripture and of the holy communion and she answered all flawlessly. When he turned his attention to me, insisting that I be as much of a guide for her as Jesus, I advised him that there would be no other who would support my Maria as much as I.

It was a quiet ceremony with just myself, Maria and Mary Anne in attendance, a request that I had made so the setting would be all the more intimate. Maria was glowing under the attention of the father, and I had to admit that though the trek had sometimes been arduous, it was worth every step to see her like this.

· · ·

Dear Caroline,

> *I'm sorry for the delay in writing to you. I hope you are well and that you haven't worried overmuch; the second half of our journey has been riddled with ill luck and I've struggled to put pen to paper and properly describe it to you without offering alarm.*

> *The ceremony in Jerusalem was incredible and awesome; Maria looked herself like a saint in her white gown, and I'm certain she glowed from within as she stood before the priest. She had to deal with her nerves to begin with, but in the end she persevered, marking one of the proudest moments of motherhood I've had thus far. I hope that she will cherish the memory of that day for all of her life.*

> *Unfortunately, our journey back home, along a different route through Damascus, was plagued with ill luck, and had the first half been as terrible, I may have taken it as an ill omen. Luckily, I don't consider omens to be anything more than a coincidence of timing, but still, it did cause me pause at times.*

> *At one point on our return home I was*

kicked by my horse, an injury that is quite aggravating and often takes rest to recover from. We did indeed take some time to rest, but thankfully I was not damaged in any major capacity and we were able to carry on after only a week or so.

The worst, for me, occurred later on.

After many allegations of misconduct and evidence to prove it, I was forced to release from my employment one of the men travelling with us. He was a fellow Italian, and so I found it difficult to do it, but I simply couldn't put up with his nuisance any longer.

Sadly, he took my actions to heart and there it festered like a poison. Shortly thereafter, he came upon me as I sat at my desk, writing a letter to you, my dear friend, and he stabbed me several times.

I've never experienced such agony as a knife slicing into me and then suddenly being pulled out. There was no pain at first, only shock and a tugging; then there was blood, so much blood.

By God's grace, Maria happened to walk in

*on the murder attempt and she was able
to scare him away. I've heard soldiers tell
me that life flashes before your eyes when
you are facing death, but I cannot agree
with them.*

*Instead, I felt the world slow down, as though
time itself had become muddied, and I
was able to think with an unexpected
clarity; I believe that was the only reason
I survived the encounter. Through my
instruction, Maria was able to perform
life saving techniques on my body that
prevented me from dying on the spot.
After she'd taken care of the worst of it, I
was treated by a doctor, and from there
was forced to rest while I recovered from
my near death experience.*

*And, dear Caroline, I wish I could tell you
that was the last of it, but I'm afraid it
isn't so.*

*Shortly after my recovery we were on our way
again, but we hadn't gotten far when
Maria came down with an illness that
left her pale, weak and feverish. Though
my own life had recently been threatened
I can say that I'd never been more afraid
than when Maria was ill.*

There were times that I was certain my words were going to be the last she ever heard, and I was careful when speaking to her, afraid that our last argument would be the thing that sent her to the other side. To make matters worse, during her time of rest we were without a home, and forced to rent a room from a man who charged an exorbitant amount of money; it was robbery, really, but I was left with no other option. Maria needed the time to recover.

I can say now with confidence that Maria will be well enough to travel again within a few days. I am hoping that the next time I write to you I will be able to do it from the comforts of my farm.

Please pray for us,
Cristina

6

MARIA, 1851-1854

Turkey

I had never been on a boat before, but I knew of them, of course, from stories: a brave captain and his trusty deckhands sail off on exciting adventures; an ambitious crew of sailors brave the dangers of the sea in order to discover new lands. As we sailed from Cyprus in the direction of Malta, I was not brave, nor was this adventure exciting.

Rather, I spent a great deal of my time with my mother, wishing that we were back in Paris or even Italy; any place other than this wretched boat would have been a welcome respite. That we weren't the only people forced from our homes was little comfort to me. I once again felt adrift, quite literally this time, and lost without a place where I could lay down roots.

Of course, I blamed my mother for all of this: it was her selfishness that had led to our upheaval; I felt certain that she cared for her country more than she cared for me, and the small child inside me refused to forgive her for that.

Here we were on another journey, a couple of refugees fleeing our own country because my mother could not behave like other mothers. Everywhere we went she insisted on becoming a part of the political atmosphere that I was certain was going to one day suffocate us. Or displace us permanently, I wasn't sure which would be the worst outcome of the two.

Our new home, it turned out, was much lovelier than I had anticipated. It was a small farm outside of Çakmakoğlu, and it was a breath of fresh air, so far as I was concerned. Before long I found myself in love with this place, as I had so inevitably fallen for each homestead we'd held before; though I didn't know it, this time would be no different than any other.

Mary Anne stayed on as my governess and was ever as strict with my studies as she'd been in Italy. She was also just as lenient with my fits of pique and melancholy moods. I could see that she felt a bit lonely out there on our farm, I was too young to appreciate properly how she must have felt in a foreign country teaching a belligerent student, and in some ways I used that loneliness to my advantage.

My mother was never one who could sit still, regardless of how content she claimed to be, and as often as not she was visiting the nearby cities. She would come back from adventures either ebulent or disturbed, it depended entirely on the company she kept and what new experiences she'd had.

"Maria, you should be ever so grateful that I didn't

bring you with me this time," she said after one such trip. "Some of the practices of Islam are despicable and disturbing, I cannot imagine how a woman could willingly allow herself to be viewed in such a manner."

"Whatever are you talking about, Mother?" I had asked. She was speaking to me as she arranged fresh sheets of paper on her writing desk and pulling out her good pen. When she spoke like this it confused me more than anything, especially because I felt that sometimes she was trying to communicate some important thought with me while holding back pertinent information.

"If it was something that you needed to know about, I would certainly ensure you were educated on the matter. As I was just saying, you should be grateful that you do not need to be told of my experience." She didn't look at me as she spoke, instead she eloquently wrote the date on the paper before her. "One can only hope that a young girl appreciates the life she has been given, understanding the life she could have been born into in other circumstances."

Then I was once more forgotten as she began her letter to her good friend in Italy. Or perhaps it wasn't a letter, but rather an essay that waxed on about her obvious superiority, something she liked to dangle in front of people whom she felt were uneducated and ignorant. I'm not sure who was more of a disappointment to the other, neither of us felt that the other was playing their role particularly well.

It annoyed me to no end that she felt I didn't have the fortitude to deal with some of the experiences she'd had, I wasn't a child anymore, I was practically a woman. Sometimes, while she was away, I would look through her notes to discover what she was trying to keep from me. It was a terrible breach of privacy, though, and I made sure never to read her letters; there were some things that I didn't want to know.

It was through my secret readings, though, that I learned more about this empire than through any conversation I'd ever had with Mary Anne or my mother. Hammams and harems were unfamiliar words and caught my attention immediately, and much to my chagrin, reading the descriptions my mother had written in her essays left me with images I couldn't shake. In some cases, I believed she was right to keep some information from me.

In other cases, I felt she was just being prudish and trying to protect me. She spoke about some of the conversations she'd had with a friend she'd met, a Lady Belmont, and the things that woman had to say were often no different than things I used to hear at my mother's soirees. It was interesting to see how naive she assumed I was after having the childhood that I did; I believe she thought she was better at hiding things than she was.

Nonetheless, after reading about some of the subjects she wrote so passionately about, I was discouraged from learning more. I decided that there were some things that a person did not need to know about in order to enjoy their life.

It was strange seeing her toiling away, doing physical labour after a life of being waited upon. Though, perhaps that wasn't fair, our lives in Paris were not always luxurious, though she did manage to make the best of any situation, whether through her wits or her acquaintances.

As a young child I had been disenfranchised with my mother and her behaviour, as I got older the feeling did not leave me, if anything it took a deeper root, like a weed that could not quite be removed. I did love her, and perhaps that was the main difficulty that I saw; I loved her and I wanted her to be the mother I felt I deserved. It was a selfish notion, but every child wishes to be the sun to their mother's Earth.

It was no surprise to me when she told me one day that she was determined for me to be baptized in the holiest of holy cities: Jerusalem. I can admit it left a bitter taste in my mouth, the idea of leaving a place that had only just started to feel like a home, just to wander the countryside so that I could be christened in a way that she felt befitted my status; truthful it was her status and her story that she wished to embellish, not my own. But I was but a child, what other option did I have than to follow her as she capered through the Ottomon Empire, studying the different cultures that surrounded her.

Mary Anne, as frustrating as she could be, was the steady, reliable person in my life. In many ways she'd become my mother by proxy and though I often gave her a hard time, I think it was because I knew that she wasn't as flighty as my own mother and when I acted out, she wouldn't run from me. My father hadn't chosen to take part in my life, and sometimes I questioned how the Princess of Independence felt about being weighed down with the responsibility of a child. It can't be something she had wanted for herself.

Though I may seem to belittle my mother for her dependence on her wealth and extravagant lifestyle, I too was guilty of the same. The tour of the empire was not an easy thing for me, what with Mary Anne insisting on offering me tutelage even while we rode, and my mother wishing to wring every last drop out of the experience that she could. To say that we were saddle sore after the first two or three weeks would have been an understatement, and I felt myself longing for more modern transportation, such as the boat that had started this adventure for us.

We were not completely alone, of course; we brought along a maid to help us with all of the necessities of travel and depending on the area, mother would hire a guide to help us through. In particular the mountain passes proved to be treacherous. I will never be able to forget the look of Femme en Rouge as she passed away in the pass of the Galileen mountains. My mother was unaware that I had secretly named each horse, and I don't believe that I disclosed my attachment to them openly, though I did grieve my Red Lady terribly.

The dervishes had also offered quite the education for me. I suspect that my mother had seen more of their ceremonies then she let on, but they were queer folk and I learned that from my own encounters with them. Mary Anne also seemed unhappy with the decision to accept their hospitality and it was her judgement that I trusted more than anyone else.

Passing into Syria had also tested my courage after my mother felt she had no choice but to hire mercenaries to ensure our safety as we made our way through the contested lands. To my mother, the insults hurled at us by the Turks were mere entertainment, to me they were the threat of violence. I found the soldiers for hire to be distasteful creatures, bent on earthly pleasures and nothing more. Mary Anne advised me to be wary of them; truth be told, I did not need her advice for that, there was a part of me that sensed the danger in them immediately.

Of all those that we met upon the way to Jerusalem, I must say my favourite was Marco de Balduci. He was a rotund man who did not seem to take himself seriously, even though he was a self-declared man of God. His brothers at the convent were welcoming and jovial, though I had assumed they would be anything but. In my experience most men who said they represented the Good Lord on this Earth were stuffy at best, usually pretentious, too.

De Balduci welcomed us into a holy land that I had never before considered entering. It was my mother's dream and I wasn't able to tell, really, how she felt about her experience. I know that at that point in our journey, I had started to appreciate my mother's goal, indeed, I was becoming willing to embrace the opportunity that she had worked so hard to bring to me.

Mary Anne was often quiet and contemplative toward the end; I think that it was more of an experience for her than either my mother or myself. I doubt that she ever imagined herself being so wide travelled when she signed on to be the governess of a bratty, spoiled child. Now she was seeing places that many wished they could visit in their lifetime.

Jerusalem, though, that was a sight to see and one I would never forget. In fact, I spent the rest of my life dreaming of that city and the emotions it brought forth inside me when we first saw it on the horizon.

I have to admit to tears when I saw myself in the

mirror in my christening gown, and I could see that my mother's eyes were also glistening. Mary Anne had not been invited to this particular outing and I sorely missed her at that moment because I felt that she had played an important role in my life as well. One that should have been recognized for what it was rather than ignored.

When mother told me that she would be coming to the christening I was delighted. Though my mother tested me in ways that only a mother could, I still craved her attention, her love and her pride; Mary Anne meant just as much to me in many of the same ways. The feelings for her were of a maternal nature, but at the same time I already knew her affection for me, whereas I could never be quite certain of my mother.

There was a tradition that had started in London called the Debutante Ball; women of high societies would arrive at the event dressed in the finest silks and cuts, and display their beauty for the world to see. That was when one knew she was a woman, and it was something that I dreamed of since I had first heard of it. After all, as the daughter of a princess, I was certain to qualify as someone of high society and the attention of all the adoring eyes around me seemed quite intoxicating.

My experience at the christening felt much the same as I had expected that ball to feel, though there were far less eyes upon me. Perhaps I felt Jesus with me that day as I stood being anointed before the priest. It was strange to experience the christening at an age where I could under-stand the significance of the ceremony; I was also at an age that would allow me to recollect that moment and the feeling of being in that fine dress before God himself, pledging myself to his service and to be true to him and his son.

Intoxicating could hardly describe the feeling.

By the time we left Jerusalem I had gone from being infatuated with the city to adoring it completely; but sadly, as with every other place of significance in my life, we had to leave it behind to continue our life elsewhere.

The journey to Jerusalem and back was quite the trek, and one that allowed me to grow not only in size but in maturity as well. I began to see the world through a different set of eyes and to understand a bit of what drove my mother. She was ever on a quest to better herself or the world around her, unable to sit still or simply enjoy a moment. To her, freedom didn't mean a life of making choices without consequences from the government, to my mother, freedom was an adventure; it was a chance to see what else was out there and to improve upon societal structures if they were found to be wanting.

We did not return back to the farm via the same route that we had travelled to Jerusalem. We visited Damascus, Aleppo and other great sights along the way. Yet still, we were fraught with ill luck for almost the entirety of our return trip.

On the morning of the murder attempt on my mother, she was in her office writing; this was her regular routine and she could often be found at that desk with a pen in hand. I cannot recall why I was on my way to see her, the very thoughts fled my head when I rounded the corner to see her lying on the floor in a pool of her own blood. The assailant stood over her, knife in hand.

I screamed out of reflex and not preservation, the man,

noticing my presence, fled the scene immediately. I dashed to my mother's side, shaking at the macabre vision before me. She had been stabbed in several places, including a wound on her neck and one on her chest.

By some miracle she remained conscious, and I can only assume it was God himself who intervened at this point.

She grasped my hand, squeezing it to get my attention; I could feel that her strength was leaving her. "Maria, listen to me," she said in a calm, though wheezy voice. "We must stop the bleeding. Put pressure on the worst of the wounds and call for help."

I did as instructed, and each step afterward as well. It was only through her sheer will and the lessons she had learned from her experience as a nurse in Italy that my mother survived, though she was never the same afterward. It took weeks for her to heal properly, and in some cases I wasn't sure she would make it back to our little farm.

It turned out that the man responsible for this attack was an employee that my mother had been forced to let go because he was guilty of several misconducts. This man, and *Italian* man, had been so wrought with emotion that he decided the only way he could right the situation was to take his revenge on my mother.

We stayed in that place for several weeks while my mother recovered from her injuries; it was difficult for we were forced to pay a ridiculous amount to rent a room from a translator, who I'm certain was aware of our dire situation and only sought to profit from it. Still we persevered, and once she was well enough to travel, we began our trek home again.

We did not traverse far before my own life force was to be tested. Whilst on the road I came down with an illness that left me incapable of standing, let alone rigorous travel. I don't remember much about the experience, except that even though she was still recovering from her own grievous injuries, she was also caring for me. The journey home tested our survival skills in ways we could have never foreseen.

My mother was kicked by her horse, stabbed, and we were forced to rent a place from a translator who sorely took advantage of our predicament. Not to mention my own illness, one that nearly took my life and required several weeks of recovery before we could continue on.

She was happy when we returned back to our farm in Çakmakoğlu. I know she enjoyed the quiet and bonding with the land, I feel that our journey to have me christened had proven to be quite enough adventure for her.

It was with bitter sadness that we returned to find that the man entrusted with our farm had not done us the service he had promised. He had absconded with mother's funds and left behind him a house in desperate need of maintenance and fallow fields. The effort required to bring our home back to its former glory was daunting and discouraging; I almost thought that mother had regretted taking off on a journey and leaving her responsibilities in the hands of a man she did not know.

She would never admit that, of course, instead she would laugh and tell me it was all part of the experience. She did not condone the behaviour of that man, and I think that should she have ever come across him he could have at least expected the rough side of her tongue, but she was too proud to admit her mistake in trusting her property to him.

It was 1853 when we returned to the farm, and immediately she began a furious effort to write to the friends she still had in Italy. She still despised the Austrians and everything they represented, but their goodwill was her only hope to recover her estates that had been confiscated due to her prior associations during the rebellion. One of her friends, Heinrich Heine, seemed to be consumed with the desire to see her return to Italy, and it was with him that she corresponded the most, though I was never privy to those letters.

Still, she remained dedicated to the farm and to the livestock we had. We were summoned to come back to Italy in 1854, but mother had requested an extension that she may reap the profit from that which she sowed and ensure the livestock were well cared for.

During our time in Turkey I had blossomed from a young girl of thirteen to a young woman at the age of seventeen. Not only had I grown as a person, I had grown spiritually and in confidence. I also benefited from my mother finally being able to legally claim me as her daughter. She had pulled some strings and was able to have me recognized as Maria Belgioso, after so many years of being considered fatherless. My feelings on the subject were mixed; as I've stated before, I craved her attention and affection, at the same time I felt myself pulling from her and wishing for a life of my own.

7

CRISTINA 1824

Italy

I can say without exaggeration that I did not live a life of physical discomfort. As a woman from a recognized family, I was expected to behave in a certain manner and accept the responsibilities of nobility. However, by 1824, the world was already moving toward democratic governments and away from the reliance on kings and queens. So, to be fair, I enjoyed a life of privilege and pleasantries with very little of the responsibilities that my ancestors before me had born.

The two most traumatic events up to this point in my life were framed by both my father and my step-father, both men who would play an intrinsic role in my values and my lifestyle. At the age of four, my father, the Marquis Jerome Trivulzio, passed away. He'd left me with a royal heritage and a royal treasury. Later my mother remarried to Marquis Alexander Visconti d'Aragona, a French nobleman, but later an Italian patriot.

My stepfather essentially had the formative years of my life, molding me with his own morality and ethics. At the age of thirteen I was witness to his arrest by the Austrians and that event shaped my life forever afterward.

The trial for my stepfather was long and drawn out, an affair of two years, that ended with his release due to lack of evidence. Still, he had been confined during the entirety of the trial, bound to a prison cell and treated like a criminal. His mental acuity was never the same upon his release, and I was forced to bear witness to his declining psychological state for the remainder of his years.

What I didn't realize at the time of his arrest was that I would experience a deep-rooted hatred of the Austrians and of the tyranny of royalty. I became more liberal in my views and instead viewed the idea of a divided Italy as one that needed to be revised, only under a ruler that had been appointed by the people of the country. If all of the states united as one, I truly believed that this was a possibility.

Thus I rebelled against my aunt at the ripe age of sixteen; it was still common at the time to have arranged marriages in an effort to ensure the legacy of the family name.

"Giorgio would be the most practical fit for you, Cristina. Your mother agrees," said my aunt Beatrice Trivulzio. She wanted nothing more than for me to wed her son and not only carry on the name but to also enhance his status in life.

"I refuse to marry a man simply because it is the best arrangement for me. A marriage arranged only to carry on a family's history and legacy is archaic at best, barbaric at worst."

"Whatever do you mean, barbaric? Your uncle and I have enjoyed a very fruitful arranged marriage and it has benefited both of us greatly."

We were in the sitting room of our estate in Milan, both of us sipping tea as though the question of my future were nothing more than an item to be checked off on an agenda. My aunt's insistence that I marry Giorgio was becoming tiresome as it was neither the first time I'd heard about it, nor was it the most convincing. Truth be told, the more my aunt and my mother insisted, the more I felt a desire to flee my responsibility to the family and do something for myself.

What the two were unaware of was my feelings for another man; one who represented the new views that were beginning to form in my young mind. Emilio Barbiano di Belgiojoso had caught my eye and from our first acquaintance I was entranced with him and his habit of generosity and charity.

I found Emilio to be an attractive man, his light hair a contrast to my own dark locks. He was funny, charming and he did not hold himself above the people, if anything he was a prince who wished he could be of the people.

I was in love, and as far as I was concerned, love was a far superior reason for marriage than what my aunt was proposing.

"I am happy that you have enjoyed a fruitful marriage but, Aunt Bee, I plan to live a life that is more than just my marriage. I don't want to just be a wife who entertains the aristocrats and tends the household. I seek a life of change, of purpose. Giorgio cannot offer me those things."

My aunt was unsettled by my candor and I could see

she was offended by my rejection of her son, but I did not let her sway me. Emilio and I would be wed, whether my family thought it was an ideal match or not; I wanted to start my life unfettered by the archaic chains of the past, Emilio and I would forge new paths and create new traditions.

"My dear Cristina, a woman at your age does not have the experience to recognize a man that has something to offer. Marry Giorgio and your children will one day sit on a throne themselves. What more could a mother hope for?"

My aunt was not being as forthright as she wanted me to believe; I know she believed that Giorgio and I would have done well together, I cannot think she would subject her son and niece to a life of misery, but she was also looking out for him. Though I could not claim any knowledge of being a mother, I knew some of the fundamentals, which were to put your child's legacy and wellbeing before any other. She may have been trying to convince me that I would benefit from a marriage to Giorgio, but in her mind she was thinking Giorgio would benefit from a union with me.

I had yet to advise anyone of my decision to marry Emilio, my interest in him was obvious even to those who spared me little of their thought, and I was concerned that I would be assaulted with reasons for me to reconsider my decision. Since my mind was settled on the matter, I didn't feel it was necessary to expose myself to the abuse.

When I spent time with him I felt alive and free from the shackles of societal expectations of women. He was a modern man with ideals that aligned with mine and represented the kind of person that I felt our world needed at the moment.

"Well, Auntie, I'm grateful for the thought and consideration that you have put into my future, but I'm afraid I must decline." I didn't meet her eye as I continued to sip on my tea. She would need a moment to recover from my bluntness on the subject and I cared enough for her that I wanted to give her that time.

"Well," she said with a sigh and slightly belligerent tone, "you are still young yet. We have time to consider your options before we make a final decision."

I bit my tongue, holding back the comment that I wished to make, though it would be unladylike and rude. I decided I would have to speak to Emilio and perhaps we would be making an announcement about our decision in the near future. "Quite true," I said.

The clock in the hall chimed the hour and I stifled a sigh of relief; Aunt Bee could not question me for the entirety of the day, I had an appointment with Ernesta Bisi. She was a beautiful woman, both in form and in life, and I admired her for far more than her artistic talent. Mother was curious where my sudden inclination for engraving had come from, but she didn't ask many questions, rather admiring Ms. Bisi's work herself.

I found Ernesta's demeanor to be fresh and quite avant-garde; inevitably our sessions often turned to political discourse at some point during my instruction and I was amazed to hear such eloquent and modern thoughts from a respected woman.

My step-father's trial and imprisonment was still a fresh wound in my heart and in my psyche, Ernesta's words helped to fuel the passion that I felt could one day dull the ache. A whole country would not be a possibility without true patriots fighting for it at every given opportunity.

Only men were able to become part of the Carbonari, a group rumoured to be dedicated to the unification of Italy under one democratic ruler, and I felt the weight of my gender wearing on me and holding me down. Ernesta helped me to see that women could also participate in the revolution of our country.

After witnessing the absolute tyranny of the Austrian rulers I knew that something must be done or others would suffer a similar fate as my stepfather. It was time for Italy to take a step forward into the modern age and put behind them such archaic anachronisms.

I placed my tea cup down on the saucer and patted my face with the linen napkin. "I enjoyed our visit today, Auntie. I'm sure mother would be happy to see you, but, unfortunately, I have an appointment for my art class to attend."

Bee scowled as she set the cup back on the saucer with a sharp click. "It's Ms. Bisi, correct?" I didn't grace her viperous tone with a response more than a smile. "I don't know why your mother thinks it's acceptable for a young woman of your stature to be under such an influence. Did you learn nothing from your stepfather?"

"I appreciate your concern, Auntie, but Ms. Bisi's political opinions are not what I seek tutelage in, it is her artwork that has caused me inspiration."

My aunt stood with a huff, tossing her napkin to the table in indignation. "You'll not want to keep her waiting."

And then she was off, likely to express her disappointment at the outcome of our conversation. I had no doubt that my mother had asked her to attempt to dissuade me from my current plans, but they underestimated my obdurate will in the matter.

I met Ernesta in the garden, a place full of greenery and beautiful colours. It was my favourite place, partially for the scenery and partly because it was generally an isolated area. My mother enjoyed her garden, but she didn't wish to spend more time with Ernesta than was required to be polite. I felt that the feeling was mutual for my instructor and so we endeavoured to have our own space for learning.

The day was bright and beautiful and I was excited to try my hand at sketching a lily, it seemed a suitable choice for two women of our persuasion. Two chairs had been set up for us in the small space and my charcoal had been laid out for me.

Ernesta was waiting for me; her fingers were black with charcoal dust and she was lost in the moment, unable to hear my steps as I approached. Still she didn't startle when she saw me, only smiled. "Cristina, you look lovely today."

I couldn't help but return the smile; I was grateful for the opportunity to escape the dreariness of my aunt and instead spend the afternoon appreciating the beauty of the world around me.

As ever, she was dressed in a practical manner, trousers and a linen shirt, it was a look that I wished I had the courage to don. My mother, though, would have an apoplexy and I'm certain that my aunt would be soon behind her.

Upon first meeting Ernesta and observing her behaviour, I immediately found myself drawn to her presence; she was a woman who didn't put up with unnecessary nonsense and treated me as an equal, rather than a superior. Equality was a feeling I quite enjoyed, preferred even, to that of the deference that I was often subjected to.

In her eyes all people had an opportunity to be great, not because they were born to some position, but rather because of their character, wit and intelligence. She made me feel like I could be something more than a pretty princess whose sole purpose was to pass down the family name and raise other children who would be expected to do the same.

"It's so good to see you," I said. "This morning was tedious." I sat down beside her and admired the strokes she'd outlined on her paper.

Like many artists, Ernesta had a knack for seeing the shapes of things rather than the whole object. Through her eyes, the world transformed into a puzzle of pieces that when put together became a thing of stunning elegance. Though my efforts were consistently improving I feared that I would never have an ability with the charcoal that she seemed to flawlessly possess.

"Tedious, you say?" She set her materials down and leaned toward me, seeming excited to hear about my morning.

"Unfortunately, yes. My aunt has done her best to convince me that I should consider a marital contract between her son and myself. Today was only one of many efforts on her part to convince me of the potential possibilities."

"How very trite," she said with a laugh. "Marriage solely as a business contract. I do hope you have better sense than that."

I nodded fervently. I could not allow, and remain comfortable with myself, this woman to believe that I was willingly partaking in this tradition. In fact, I felt quite the opposite, straining since I was a young child against the restrictions that my own family confined me with. "I haven't said anything, I've been waiting for an opportune moment, but I have another man in mind."

"Oh?" she said, picking up her charcoal again. "Who might this young man be? Anyone I know?"

"I would assume that you've at least heard his name in the circles that you travel in." I carefully ran my fingers over the different chunks of charcoal in front of me, wishing to pick the one that felt right. "I plan to wed Emilio Barbiano di Belgiojoso."

"The prince?" she asked, sending a brief glance in my direction.

"He is a prince, but like me, he doesn't hold to the old traditions. He looks to the future and chooses to spend his time and his funds in the pursuit of those ideals."

"I've heard that he can be quite generous."

I pulled the charcoal down the paper, imitating the lines of the lily. The star-shaped flower was treasured by all Italians, regardless of their nation; it was therefore my favourite flower. "It is that quality in particular that first attracted me to him," I confessed. "He can be quite charming, but he is also selfless."

I was to see Emilio that evening and I was looking forward to the meeting, in spite of the fact that it was to be done in secrecy. Tonight I planned to speak to him of marriage. I couldn't stand the thought of spending another tea time considering the options that were available to me, as my aunt had so kindly worded it.

"I'm sure you two will make a handsome couple," she said.

My feeling of euphoria and excitement was bolstered by the statement and I found myself unable to concentrate on the sketch. She offered me some constructive criticism, but I was so focused on my evening plans that little of it really remained with me. I was certain she secretly believed that I was nothing more than a foolish girl chasing after the dream of love at that point, but I could hardly bring myself to care.

Ernesta allowed me to see a world outside of the stark role into which I had been born. I knew that she spent time with members of the Carbonari, and I hated to admit it, but I was envious. To me her life was quite romantic: an artist married to a wealthy man that she loved, involved in the political revolution of a united Italian nation. On top of all of this, she had managed to fulfill her familial duty by producing five children, a thought that daunted me at the best of times.

If Ernesta, as a woman, could define herself as someone who chose to make changes to society and someone who also chose to appreciate the beauty of the world around us, then why should I not pursue a similar path. In my dear art tutor I saw the possibility of a future of my own, unrestrained and glorious.

8

MARIA, 1854

Turkey

*A*s a result of her own personal failures in the world of marriage, my mother put very little stock in the institution. Her marriage had not succeeded in the way she had hoped and she'd had nothing of significance romantically since then. She didn't even speak of my father, who should have arguably been one of the most important men in her life.

So it was no surprise that when I started receiving the attention of a grown man, an artist, she was quite discomforted. I believe there was genuine fear in her heart when she told me that this man was of no consequence and should not entrance me as he did. Her lack of interest only flamed the fires of my heart and I felt myself drawn to him all the more.

It was possible that he wasn't extravagant enough for her liking, he seldom picked subjects that would cause a politically infused conversation. I would agree with her there, his paintings were not exciting or controversial and perhaps that's why I was drawn to them; they represented the exact opposite of my mother.

I had insisted on an art tutor to round out my education; Mary Anne was an excellent scholar and I adored her, but she was unskilled when it came to the visual representation of beauty in our world, something she admitted herself. My mother had offered to give me her own guidance initially, after all, she'd trained with the great Ernesta Bisi. After several sessions it became obvious that she and I were not meant to discuss the finer details of art, let alone as a teacher and student relationship.

We decided the only solution was to hire someone to come live nearby so that I may have regular lessons. My mother had several tutors come to the farm for interviews and I requested to join her and participate in the process. At first she was delighted that I was showing interest in ensuring that we hired the teacher with the best skill set; however, I'm certain that she soon grew weary of my unending questions and insistence in certain areas.

"Maria, certainly the tenor of his voice doesn't play a role in his ability to paint," she said after one meeting. I had rejected the candidate out of hand as soon as he'd walked out the door. She'd thrown her hands up in the air, seemingly defeated by my attitude toward all of the prospective teachers.

"You are not the one who is going to have to listen to a nasally voice, are you?" I liked to believe that I was being particular for perfectly just reasons, but looking back I suspect that I was instead trying to insert some kind of control over my life. I was sixteen and looking toward a future of independence; after all, my mother had married at sixteen.

"Sometimes you have to endeavour to look past the minor irritations of a person's characteristics in order to find someone with true talent. In fact, those who do have talent often lack the social grace that other people have."

"I didn't like his artwork, either."

"Why not?"

"He's too modern, I would like to learn the classics from someone."

Though I argued with her for quite some time on the subject she advised me to choose someone soon or she would make the choice arbitrarily and I may not be pleased with the result. Her insistence on haste annoyed me, but not enough for me to push any further, my mother always kept her word, especially in regards to discipline.

In the end we decided that my education in art would continue to be offered by Mary Anne. I was not amenable to her making the choice on my account and she refused to sit through another interview with me.

A few weeks later one of the men returned to the farm under the guise of inquiring as to whether the position was still open. It was late when he arrived, so my mother felt obligated to invite him to join us for dinner, though I could see that she would rather see him on his way.

I couldn't recall the reason I'd given mother for not wanting him to teach me, but it seemed unimportant now that he'd returned; especially when it became clear that he wasn't interested in the teaching position.

"Are you in the habit of inquiring about all of your job prospects personally?" my mother asked over a dinner of fish and rice.

He blushed slightly at her remark, making his pale cheeks turn a remarkable rosy colour. I wasn't sure why, but I felt the urge to look away as soon as I saw the blush, and I was unable to look at him again while he responded.

"If I'm being honest, Your Majesty, my presence here is not due entirely to the available position."

"Oh?" came her response. He was unaware of where her emotions were heading based on her tone, but I could feel it and I racked my brain trying to find a topic that would be less dangerous for the man.

"I returned because I was quite entranced by Maria. I know now that she rejected me as a tutor, but I was wondering if she would decline an invitation for a walk." At the look he received from my mother he quickly added, "Chaperoned, of course."

She didn't respond to him immediately, and I wasn't certain if she was hoping that I would speak up, but I didn't look; I could feel myself blushing as well. I was surprised how flattered I felt at the request, after all, I had rejected him only days prior.

After a prolonged silence filled only with the scraping of plates, my mother finally deigned to respond. "If Maria wishes to spend time with you, Master De Luca, then I would not be opposed to a suitable rendezvous. However, I feel that you should afford her some time to consider your offer, this evening would be a bit… rushed."

"I would be delighted," I said immediately. The look she sent in my direction was one I didn't want to see, I'm sure there was poison in that look.

He smiled at me and took a sip of his wine; I was certain he was buying time to consider an appropriate response considering my mother's presence. "Then I shall return at your earliest convenience," he said.

"Thank—" started my mother, but I interrupted her, furthering her frustration with me.

"Tomorrow, Master De Luca."

"Maria!" There was a bite to her tone, and I looked down at my plate again. "Rudeness is not acceptable in any circumstance. You are being inconsiderate to both me and our guest. Do you recall the length he has had to travel simply to visit you?"

She was right, of course, but my excitement at having a man interested in me had quite overrun my senses.

"It was not as terrible as it seems," he said. He was trying to placate her and douse her temper before it truly caught. "I can come at midday, if that would be acceptable."

I could tell by her pinched expression that she was not at all pleased with how this conversation was playing out. She gave him a brief smile that didn't seem to reach her eyes and said, "Midday would be acceptable."

And so I started one of the most exciting periods of my life to date; my mother didn't appreciate the way his presence eclipsed all other desires for me and she was quick to caution me. But when he came that first day with a single tulip, I thought that my chest wouldn't be able to contain the emotions that coursed through me.

He came to visit several times over the next couple of weeks; each time my mother insisted on chaperoning us herself, filling our conversation with her witty quips and observations. Just when it seemed we would have a moment to speak, just the two of us, she would interrupt with some comment about the political climate of the empire.

Eventually, Antonio brought me a painting of a single orange tulip on a blue background. My mother fawned over the work until Antonio was on his way home, and then she expressed her true opinion of the work.

Regardless of how my mother belittled Antonio, I found my feelings growing more acute with each visit and she could see that in my eyes. Her fear that I might actually consider marrying this man grew with each walk through our gardens; she could say little without sounding like a hypocrite, given her decisions at my same age.

Instead, she made the choice to show me the mistake she thought I would be making if I devoted my life to the painter. I have to admit that when she told me that I would be accompanying her to a soiree, I was initially excited; I didn't know the true purpose of the evening and my mother could be very conniving when she wanted to be.

The salon we visited was in Ankara, where mother had made an acquaintance with the type of people she normally did: artists, musicians, patriots and thinkers. I felt uncomfortable from the very beginning of the event, though my mother seemed to meld into the crowd, seeming inseparable from the talent that surrounded her.

There was wine and hors d'oeuvres and women dressed

both lavisciously and scandalously. On more than one occasion I found myself blushing at the sights before me, and I know that my mother drew some pleasure from my discomfort.

I was never far from her side, fearing that I would be drawn into a conversation that I couldn't follow; I considered myself educated, but hardly worldly despite the many homes I'd had.

"Antonio De Luca?" I heard a man say to my mother. I immediately felt my ire rise, her ruse was beginning to become clear and I wasn't going to put up with it quietly. "I think the man would travel to the ends of the Earth for the attention of a lady."

The comment made me swallow my acerbic words that I had intended to aim in my mother's direction. "What do you mean?" I said instead.

The man grinned lasciviously and then made a dramatic point of looking around the room, "Let's just say that many a woman here has spent some time with our dear painter."

For the first time I looked around the room without the cloud of emotion that I had felt with Antonio. The men and women were all behaving in a way that would not pass at a dinner table; in fact, I had the sense that if we stayed much longer we would see even more flesh being unveiled.

The women all smirked at the men, drawing their attention to their bosom whenever possible and laughing gayly at the humorous anecdotes the men made. In one case there were three women fawning over one man in a manner that promised much more than they were currently offering.

I was having difficulty breathing as I looked around the room with dismay. "Maria?" asked my mother with a voice filled with concern. "Are you going to faint?"

I shook my head, but I turned and looked for the door. Once I was making my way through the crowd toward it, my mother fell into place behind me, offering niceties to those who spoke to her. She was a master of conversation, leaving laughter following behind her.

When we were finally able to leave the building, I felt myself gasping breaths of the fresh evening air, gulping them down like a man who had been trapped in a desert would drink water. "Why did you bring me here?" I demanded.

My mother touched my arm and the look she gave me was one of pity, and I wasn't sure whether I should be offended or saddened. "My husband spent time at many soirees like this one. In the beginning it was exciting, liberal and so different from the life that I had been raised in. My family had warned me time and again against the decision to marry Emilio, but whenever I would see him my feelings would cover my common sense and I would forget what they had said to me.

"I know how Antonio makes you feel, Maria. I know that you walk on air when he's near, time stops and no one else enters your thoughts. Every time he smiles you try to remember what you'd done to make him do that so you can repeat it.

"I know that you find my presence to be a thorn in your side and that you desire just one moment alone with him so you can see if his lips are as soft as they look." She pulled me into an embrace that made me feel like a small child again.

I had wanted to protest all of her words, but their truth rang in my head and my heart and I could not in good conscience deny it. Antonio did all of those things with me, and if that gentleman was to be believed, he did that for many women.

"I don't doubt that Antonio has feelings for you, my sweet girl. I can't imagine what else would possess him to make that trek so often, it certainly isn't my company. But it's not in his nature to remain true to you in the way that you desire."

I had imagined a life with Antonio; in my dreams I had been his wife and bore his children. Seeing this side of him, one that I likely would not have been exposed to before I made the decision to marry him if not for my mother, it made me reconsider what my life would look like.

Being the wife of a libertine would be a humiliating experience, would I be able to stand it? My own mother had left her husband for similar behaviour and her life had not been an easy one. Granted, some of her choices were responsible for that, but I couldn't imagine what it would be like to be alone with a child who relied on you for everything. A child who could very well resent you at some point.

"I would like to go home," I said in response. Antonio was due to come the next day and I decided that I would send someone else out to greet him and turn him away. Though I recognized that my heart was beginning to harden against him, I didn't trust myself to resist the temptation of just one kiss or one last smile.

It hurt to admit to myself that she was right, but it was a necessary growing process for me. I shudder to think what my life would have been like had she not made the effort to convey that message to me.

9

CRISTINA 1830-1840

Paris

 t was horrendously difficult to admit to myself that my family had been correct about Emilio. The first few months had been lovely and intriguing; my naivety, though, was more than I had believed it ever could be, and I witnessed this first hand as I watched Emilio in scandalous circles.

Still, I believed he would remain true to me, and in my certainty I once again showed my youth. Emilio was incapable of being true to me and it had been silly and romantic of me to assume that he could. Once I spent more time in the circles he frequented, I realized that a life with him was not one I was willing to live, much less bring up a child in.

For his part, though, I have to say that he was not cruel to me, nor did he cause me any physical distress, he was just simply unable to deny himself the opportunities of the lifestyle to which he was accustomed. Our friendship remained intact, but when it became clear that I was uninterested in his hobbies, we went our separate ways, neither one offended by the other.

Instead, I spent more and more time with Ernesta. She had gone beyond art teacher, and had become a dear friend of mine. The more I learned about her, the more I wanted to spend my time with her and learn from her.

She was an interesting woman: a patriot, artist and active revolutionary. These were all things that I felt were true about myself as well. More and more often I would find myself by her side as the days went on, especially if I didn't want to accompany Emilio to one thing or another.

Ernesta always seemed happy to have me by her side for these events and I slowly found myself immersed in a political world that had not previously been known to me. Through Ernesta I was introduced to revolutionaries in the Carbonari and I learned where I could invest finances to help further the cause of the Italian Revolution.

It was an exciting time to live in, all around us history was being made. In France, the revolution gave us hope and two of the Carbonari, Ciro Minotti and Enrico Misley, sought to use the energy in France to help our dear country grow to be something more.

I met these two at different events; I was always entranced by their passion and indeed struggled with keeping my emotions in order whenever I heard them speak. Ernesta was good friends with the two of them, but as women we could not be members of the Carbonari. Wishing to still be a part of the revolution, I became a gardineri.

Through the gardineri I was able to ensure that funds

reached the right people to help further their hold of their area.

When the Duke of Mordana turned on Misley and Minotti, it was a blow to our cause. We had trusted our neighbours to help us gain the freedom they had. Instead Mordana turned the two into the Austrian government.

Still, parts of the Italian states were carrying on with the fighting. The revolt went from Romagna to all of the other papal states with the exception of Lazio. Unfortunately their lack of organization and the lack of the follow through from the French led to the early demise of our attempt to unify our country.

In 1831, the Austrian military marched through, ending any further fighting that threatened to change the current course of the government.

Unfortunately, due to my efforts with the gardineri and my friendship with Ernesta, I was someone that the military was watching. I had my own circle of influence and had become one of the known revolutionaries who could be a threat to the current state.

I was both proud of this and a little frightened; to be seen as a figure that participated in the efforts to unify Italy democratically was an honour that I wished I could share with my stepfather. On the other hand, if I was being spied on I had to be careful that I did not misstep in any way that could lead to my own arrest. I had seen how the trials of those who were arrested could drag on; I wanted no part of that.

Though we had been defeated once, there were still those who were unwilling to let things return to the norm most had come to accept. Giuseppe Mazzini was one who was more than ready to see his dream be a reality. He rejected the unorganized Carbonari and started his own group that he vowed would be more prepared to follow through with their plans: Giovine Italia.

Forced into exile, Mazzini still organized another revolt in an attempt to unite Italy as one republic. He saw quite the success, with over sixty thousand adherents to it in its prime. Unfortunately the Savoy government became aware of his plot before it was to take place there and his revolution was crushed.

The attention I was receiving from the Austrian spies placed me in a predicament that I had not ever imagined myself to be in. I was forced to flee my home without a penny.

I arrived in Paris in 1831, and thanks to my estranged husband I was able to afford some accommodations close to the Madeleine. It was a small apartment, and I learned quickly how little I knew of the working world as I struggled to provide for myself.

It was one thing for me to be aware of the value of coins as part of my education. I could tell anyone what a silver coin from any country was valued at, but I couldn't tell you how much bread I could buy with five francs.

This was a part of life that I had not seen before, having lived a life of luxury and wealth. There were always others who looked after the mundane tasks of cooking and cleaning, it was an astounding and humbling experience for me. I was unprepared for the lifestyle I could afford and was thankful when my husband was kind enough to extend me further funds that helped me to purchase a salon.

During my life in Milan I'd learned how to attract the attention of those around me and how to ensure that they had a lasting impression that I wanted them to have. One common refrain I'd heard used to describe me was that I was pale as a ghost. It was said in contempt and I'm sure those who uttered the phrase did not hold any affection for me, but I decided that I would become the thing they thought me to be.

My pale skin, dark eyes and black hair were the features that stood out the most to those around me. I wanted my salon to be a reflection of myself and my never ending devotion to the cause I had fought for, therefore I created a salon that represented the best Italy had to offer. I filled my space with paintings from the renaissance, brilliant colours and gave it a romantic atmosphere. When people thought of me, I wanted them to think of Italy, and not my skin or hair.

An introductory letter from a friend, Augustin Thierry, I was able to make the acquaintance of the French Foreign Minister, François Mignet. Not only was François charming and witty, he was also one of the founders of Le National, a local paper.

François and I developed a deep friendship, both being of a similar disposition when it came to politics and art and it was through him that I was able to meet many others in the local political sector in Paris. I found my tendencies aimed toward musicians in particular, as they had always fascinated me; I confess that I have no abilities in the area, and surrounding myself with those who were brilliant with music seemed the best alternative.

I also made the friendship of Gilbert de Lafayette, a

man of the French military and a revolutionary like myself. I appreciated his maturity and found him to be a comforting presence during my time in Paris.

The only woman I was able to make strong ties with was Caroline Jaubert; she was a dear friend and one whose opinion I treasured.

The independence of my nation was still my main passion, though, and everything I did was because I wished to further that goal for my country. When I'd first made my way to Paris I was on my own except for some funds from my estranged husband. As time grew on, more and more Italian patriots sought refuge in Paris and they held my heart and my interest more than anything else.

Having known what it was like to be destitute in a country that was not native to you, I worked tirelessly to help those refugees who fled Italy for Paris. My soirees were well known throughout Paris, and I invited many French diplomats or other members of the French government; I also ensured to bring in those Italian countrymen who were new to France. Thus I was able to help them make the connections they needed to find their footing in a foreign land.

My efforts to reunite Italy never stopped while I was in Paris; if I wasn't helping out my fellow countrymen then I was raising funds and writing letters in the hopes of accomplishing something. Unfortunately, my finances were not where I wished them to be. The Austrians had seized control of my estate, requiring me to return home within their given time period or be declared dead and lose everything.

Naturally, I did not bend the knee nor grovel and beg

for forgiveness; I was surviving in Paris and I knew that their possession of my property would only be for a short period of time. Mazzini was working tirelessly to promote Young Italy, and I was grateful that he felt that I was one who could further the cause after the failure of the Carbonari.

When he told me that he was writing an open letter to Charles Albert—currently the leader of Sardinia—about taking the throne for a united Italy, I was initially thrilled. Charles Albert seemed to have similar feelings in regards to our country and it was exciting to feel like one was on the cusp of historical changes.

Mazzini and I exchanged many correspondences during my time in Paris; I was well connected with those that had influence in France, and I was able to secure promises from many that they would support the rise of Charles to the throne. How invigorating it was to be in the epicenter of political intrigue in Paris.

Learning that Charles had decided to lean toward his Christian character was disappointing for us all; most of all the French who had promised to back him should he unify the country. The influence of the pope and other religious figures had been too much, and Charles felt that it would indeed not be best for the country if he were to ascend the throne.

In my opinion, it had been decided that it was not in the best interest of the church that he bring Italy together, but that is neither here nor there.

I knew that the Austrians were still spying on me, but I didn't care; I was always discreet, as were my patrons, so I felt quite secure in the knowledge that the Austrians would gain nothing by trying to watch me. I was a socialite and that was all; I held extravagant parties at my salon and I was greatly admired by many Italians and those of the French ministry. I was well placed to help Mazzini with his cause.

Adolphe Tiers, a French statesman I befriended, was a frequent guest of mine, and though I was certain that he was hoping for more than I was willing to offer, his presence was nevertheless welcomed.

"My dear Cristina, I would be delighted if you would allow me to prepare an omelette for you. It would be perfect paired with a nice wine," he said one evening after the guests had all made their way home. Tiers would often linger, waiting for the opportunity to talk to me alone and I encouraged it, the influence he held was strategic for me.

"An omelette? I do not believe I've ever had one of your omelettes." I wasn't sure if I'd ever eaten one, but my understanding was that Tier could have been a chef had he answered the calling and who was I to decline good food when it was freely offered to me?

"And mine are simply divine," he said with a suggestive smile.

I wondered what he expected in return for the eggs; I wasn't yet sure the price I was willing to pay for anything; some men requested an extreme price indeed for small favours like that.

"Well, then," I said with a grin, "Why should I be the only one to taste it? I shall have a party and have someone come to play the piano for us." In my mind I was already assembling a guest list. François of course, Lafayette, and there were some patriots that I'd heard of as well and I

would extend an invitation to them. For the entertainment though, there was a young man who I felt was quite
talented and I wondered if he would be interested in
playing for us.

"A party?" he asked. I could see he was disappointed
but he hid it well; it was only experience that allowed me
to see it.

"Yes, one in your honour, of course," I said. "I believe
that something as decadent as your food should be experienced by many, not just I." Inflating a man's ego was not
something that I had difficulty with, I had long since been
aware of the effect of my body on the male mind and I
was willing to use anything I could to my advantage.

Of course, after such fawning on my part he could
hardly refuse my offer and I was pleased with my effort to
give him what he wanted without cornering myself into a
situation that I didn't want.

It was through conversations like the one with Tiers
that really allowed me to bring together the greats. During
my time in the salon I spent my hours surrounded by
greatness and achievement and it was not a life that I
would willingly trade for anything else.

Over time I went from entertaining guests and intro-
ducing them to holding charity events so that I might raise
funds for the cause. My acclaim was such that few people
would decline an invite to one of my gatherings and,
indeed, many would see attending one of my soirees as an
opportunity to increase their social status.

Therefore I was able to bring some truly brilliant
minds together. François, as always, remained my stalwart
companion during my endeavours, and it was his compan-

ionship that I craved the most; a night of privacy with him was always a sensual delight.

He and Lafayette were my closest companions at the time, and once my dear friend Lafayette passed, there was only François. More often than not he would remain at my salon long after others had left, often outlasting Tiers, to my benefit.

"You are so beautiful, my princess," he said one evening, taking me in his arms and pressing his lips to mine. As usual, I was dazzled with his presence and his charm, unable to resist him.

François was not the only lover I had over time, but he was the one that was dearest to my heart; though I was still married to Emilio, I wished to spend my time with François instead.

In 1837 I decided to host an event that I knew would make my previous events seem tedious and monotonous; I had news of some Italian immigrants who needed financial aid whilst in France and I decided to host a gathering to raise funds for them.

Due to my forward nature and my lack of guile, I made friends who were talented, not necessarily wealthy or descending from old blood. Thus I was able to find talent in the places that many of my social stature would not have noticed, having failed to give equal opportunity to every man.

When I hosted the bazaar, I contacted several of my acquaintances that sold artwork: Eugene Delacroix, Ary Scheffer, Edward Grenet and Paul Delaroche. Each of them, amongst others, agreed to donate some of their artwork to the cause, which were sold during the evening.

I also invited Franz Liszt, Frederic Chopin and Sigismond Thalberg.

I felt the evening was a success from the very beginning, there was a gay atmosphere and a general jovility throughout the salon. As part of the entertainment I arranged a Hexameron, a piano and several composers created pieces for the part. It was unfortunate that it was not ready to be played at my salon on the night of the bazaar, but I was more than intrigued with it and followed its development afterward.

The evening was an utter delight for me; I felt that I was part of something larger than we could all know. All of the paintings sold and I was both grateful for the donated funds and happy for the artists whose work would now be proudly on display in someone's homes.

All of the pianists spent some time tickling the keys, ensuring all of my guests were entertained. After much applause two pianists, Liszt and Thalberg started taking turns at the piano and it became apparent that a piano duel had begun.

There was much cheering, and in some discreet ways I suspect that there were wagers placed on who the winner would be.

"Your Majesty," said Chopin, "You must be the one who decides the winner." I noticed that those in the near area were looking to me.

"Why on Earth do you say that?" I asked, feeling a bit shy about the prospect and a little nervous at potentially offending one of my guests, though they seemed to be both in good spirits.

"As our hostess and the most beautiful woman in the room, there can be no other," he insisted.

François stood beside me and whispered in my ear, sending shivers of desire down my spine. "Certainly you are the most qualified to decide who was most successful, you have an ear for music and a knack for reading the crowd." I smiled at him and placed a hand on his arm, a promise for later.

"Very well, I shall be the one to make the decision. Now lets be done with the talking and let the music speak for itself."

Each of the men seemed to become even more passionate about their performance, if that was even possible. Their music increased in pace and crescendo, becoming intricate and complex; it was an astounding performance from both.

When finally they were finished, I confess I had to think for a moment before I could declare anything. Both of these men were extremely talented and both deserved high praise. However, I couldn't go without naming one greater than the other, I had been requested to be a judge.

Finally I stood and tapped my glass to get everyone's attention. "I've never been serenaded by such skillful hands as I have tonight," I said. "Of course, while both men know well how to play the piano, I have been requested to make a decision about whose performance was the greatest, and so I shall.

"Thalberg is the best pianist in the world; Liszt is the only one." Both men took deep bows and the applause in the room was near deafening.

I was happy to see that the competition did not seem

to affect the camaraderie between the two, and was indeed pleased to know that they continued their friendship later on.

François leaned down and said over the noise, "I look forward to publishing your essay about your thoughts on this duel. The National has benefited from your words."

In 1838 my life changed irrefutably; though I had been careful, I found myself with child; a position that I had rarely imagined myself in. The father was not Emilio, and who it was beyond that didn't matter; my daughter Maria was born out of wedlock, but as a modern woman, I did my very best to ensure that didn't affect her negatively.

10

MARIA 1856-1861

Italy

$\mathscr{I}$ could see that mother was not as confident about her return to Italy as she was wont to say; I rather think that she was afraid of the backlash she would receive upon her return. People can be cruel, and those who disliked my mother did so viciously.

However, our return was not one she needed to concern herself with; we arrived back in Milan without any issues and I was very grateful for it. Life in Turkey had been quiet and peaceful, but it wasn't Italy and it most certainly wasn't Paris.

Since my mother had helped me to realize the mistake I would be making by marrying Antonio, I had grown more inclined to regard the things she said to me with respect. I was temperamental and obdurate during my childhood, often punishing her for what I perceived were misdeeds, but in fact they were only the acts of a mother trying her best.

When we returned I watched my mother blossom once more; no longer did she need to toil at providing food for her family, instead she could work toward her true passion: uniting Italy.

During the first years of our return we stayed with my dear Aunt Theresa, she was my mother's half-sister and junior by fourteen years, yet I could see she adored my mother. After spending so much time on our own, I found myself comforted to be surrounded by familial blood, and I could see that my mother did as well.

Though my aunt did not have the same intellectual opinions as my mother, the two had more in common than I would have imagined my mother could have with a domesticated wife. It was refreshing to see the change come over her and to see her joy around her sister. In many ways I wished that I had a similar bond with a sibling, but alas, it was never to be so.

Eventually the efforts of my mother's good friend Heinrich Heine were able to convince the Austrians to release her property and we were able to return to Milan and our original home.

I was now a woman, no longer a child, and I found myself looking at the world around me with new eyes. No more did I feel the petulant desire to judge or punish my mother, or at the very least it was dramatically reduced.

Instead, I found myself seeing the world through her eyes more and more everyday. As I spent time in Italy I saw the privilege into which I'd been born, despite our hardships and occasional circumstance. Those who were not as privileged as I, struggled and toiled on a daily basis to provide a meager wage for their family.

I also paid more attention to the difference of how those not born of a well-known family were treated as opposed to someone like myself. It hardly seemed fair that I should receive preferential treatment for simply having been born to my mother.

In February 1858, my mother's husband, Emilio, passed away at the age of fifty-seven. I could see that my mother mourned him in her own way, as the two had remained cordial during their marriage, if not intimate. Otherwise, my mother carried on with her singular passion, that of the unification of her country.

For quite some time she had been disenfranchised with Mazzini's Young Italy, and now cared not how the country was ruled, only that it was ruled by Italians. She was ever fastidious with her writing and her meetings, insisting on playing a role in Italy's revolution regardless of how it took place.

As I grew into a young woman, I found myself caring for the same things she did and following in her footsteps. I, too, began putting whatever abilities I had to work for the country.

Though I was a young woman experiencing my country through new eyes, my mother was not as young as she used to be. After her near death at the hands of a man in our service, she had never been the same. Gone was her straight posture and her confident head held high, instead she seemed to be in pain at all times. Sometimes I noticed that her gait seemed slower, almost a shuffle and she never held her head as high again.

It was perhaps those things that helped me to realize what my mother had attempted to accomplish in her life.

Who was I to pass judgement on the way she had responded to the trials and tribulations she had endured. She had not been young when she had me and had lived a full life up until that point; it could not have been easy for her to become a mother first and a revolutionary second.

But still, her refusal to let the issue go was inspirational to me; she had been exiled, penniless and worse, but yet she would not bow down to the Austrians and admit defeat.

After she began to see that Mazzini's Young Italy would not be ideal, my mother attached herself to another man who had the ear of Napoleon III. Camillo Cavour didn't like the concept behind Mazzini's idea for creating one Italy. Mazzini had been of the opinion that a revolution was necessary in order to foist the current rulers out and bring in one man, Charles Albert, to rule the country as a whole.

When Charles chose not to unite the country it was a bitter disappointment, and perhaps even defeat for Young Italy.

Instead Cavour favoured the idea that small changes in government would instead create the foundation for change. My mother, a skilled manipulator and well-connected woman, was immediately recognized as an asset, and Cavour worked with her to ensure the future of the country.

It was not only those two who craved a change in the regime; civil unrest was extremely high, and soldiers were required to deal with angry citizens on a daily basis. My mother saw this, too, and I often wondered if it caused her as much pain as her physical injuries had caused her.

More and more I wished to spend time with her, learning what I could and helping her to achieve her dream; I could see that was becoming a reality. With each small plot or intrigue with Cavour, my mother managed to work toward bringing the Italian states together.

She had nearly as much political influence on the matter as any politician or general, and I found myself admiring her now more than ever because of the qualities that had made this possible. Somehow, though I resisted and fought as much as I could as a child, she managed to make a revolutionary out of me, and I knew that I would dedicate my life to the same cause as she.

11

CRISTINA, 1860

Italy

I had expected to return to my home with the criticism of many voices surrounding me; I was pleased to find that this was not the case. During my life, I had received the highest of praises from others and the most hideous of insults as well.

My leavetaking had not been without scandal; there were many things that occurred after I fled that caused the tongues of jealous women to wag, I could not change that. Yet, I didn't want the joy of my homecoming to be marred by such words, nor did I want to expose my daughter to the hatred she would have to endure.

I was overjoyed to finally have Maria legitimized. I always knew that I would eventually do it, but sometimes I had feared that I would not be able to do it in my lifetime.

The death of Emilio was not easy; we'd had our issues and we did not have a conventional marriage, yet he represented a part of me that I could no longer revisit. With his death all I had were memories from those times.

I was not the same person now as I had been when I fled my home for the quiet of the Turkish countryside. I had endured more there than I had elsewhere and it changed me physically, nearly sucking my youth out of me and ensuring that I would never again hold my head high.

The wound on my neck had healed such that I couldn't lift my head straight, I forever had it bent and it galled me that I might be giving the impression of meekness or deference, for it was neither of those things.

If anything, I felt stronger than I was before, my convictions were rooted deeply and I would not be distracted from them.

I noticed a change in Maria as well; no longer was she a child who hated her mother for moving her around from one place to the other. It seemed that she recognized the work of my life and all that I had sacrificed for my country; if anything she was more interested in my efforts than she had been before.

Looking back, I realized that Mazzini's efforts to unite my country had been a mistake; while the man had vision, he had been too young to realize how the changes needed to be made. It was unfortunate that he had intentionally surrounded himself with a younger generation that did not have the fortitude and patience to try anything but force.

I was fortunate to meet a man named Camillo Cavour, he had the ear of Napoleon, was the Prime Minister of Piedmont and had aspirations that were aligned with my own. Cavour was subtle where Mazzini had been rash and imperturbable where the other had been quick to emotions.

Cavour and I formed a bond over a mutual goal for our country and we spent many hours together working out how we could make the states unite. I met with him during the morning hours as he travelled around and we had many conversations.

Some of the conversations were about inconsequential things, but normally we were plotting; he had recognized in me someone who could connect with important people. Through family, marriage and my experiences in Paris, I was able to bring him in touch with all the necessary players for true change.

Over time, Cavour and I were able to slowly take the necessary steps to improve our situation. Cavour remained the man that everyone saw, while I worked in the shadows, pulling strings and reaching out to those in other states that I knew.

I was quite content to not be center stage for this coup; too many times I had been the person under watch for my potential to cause issues for Austria. I now appreciated the anonymity of being hidden, though I'm sure there were officials who were aware of everything I did. I don't believe that I would ever be someone they took for granted or overlooked, though I might have been older, I was every bit as capable as I had been.

The unrest in Italy had been somewhat encouraging when I returned. It seemed to me that the people were at their own crossroads, trying to decide which direction to turn in; there were some, I know, who didn't wish to see conflict anymore, and others who thirsted for it.

I was far past the time of thirsting for blood; I simply wanted peace.

In 1861, Victor Emmanual II declared the Kingdom of Italy. Our dreams and our hard work had finally born the sweet fruit of freedom.

Cavour was the first prime minister of the country, and he had much work ahead of him. When he'd first become Prime Minister of Piedmont, he'd only had a small area that he looked after; now he had five times that amount and the rules had all changed. Now he was tasked with forming the foundation of a new country that would fairly represent our people.

I had felt a restlessness for the entirety of my life up until that point. It had begun when I was but a child and witness to the damage that foreign rulers could do to our family. My step-father's own trials became the fuel for the fire of my passion.

Once we'd succeeded in our goal, I felt that fire start to fade and for the first time looked around me to see what I had missed while I had been working so tirelessly. It was a strange feeling to achieve a dream and not know which direction to walk in next, but I embraced it.

Dearest Caroline,

> *Today is a day of pure joy for me. I have been working my entire life toward this moment and cannot be more pleased to see it arrive. It has taken years of sacrifice and toil, but finally our country can be*

united as one, and those outsiders can be ousted from their perches.

It's a strange feeling to achieve your dream. At first it's exaltation and elation you feel as though your feet will never again touch the ground and your head will never sit below the clouds again. Then there is a feeling of weariness so strong that you begin to wonder if you will ever rise again.

I'm sure that tomorrow I shall wonder what to do with myself, but for today, I'm choosing to celebrate. Maria is of course happy, but I don't think she shared the same enthusiasm for this moment as I did; I suspect much of that is because of the way that she was raised, as though this wasn't just a possible reality, but the only reality. Whereas, I was raised with only the hope that this one day might be achieved.

I've been hesitant to say anything to you, but upon my return to Italy, I became just as active in the unification of Italy as I had been before I was forced to flee. This time I was even more discrete, though, wishing to live out the remainder of my life in my

*homeland rather than as a refugee
elsewhere.*

*My hard work has paid off and today we are
looking at a country that will be ruled by
a leader elected by the people and all will
be able to have a say, regardless of their
societal status.*

*I hope that on this day you are feeling just as
I am, because this is a tremendous
accomplishment for all of our people.*

Sincerely,
Cristina

12

MARIA, 1860 FORWARD

Italy

W hen I had been younger, before meeting the man I love, I had planned to follow in my mother's footsteps, furthering one cause or another. Then I met Marquis Ludovico and everything in my world changed.

My children were going to live a life far different than my own; it would be one with a reliability and security that I had never known. My mother had fought to give my children, and many other children, that security.

However, that didn't mean she had changed as a person; she was still the modern woman insisting that I not give in to social conventions and instead forge a new path in the world. I'd watched my mother do that my entire life and I wanted something different for myself.

When I agreed to marry Ludovico, my mother was aghast, certain that she had shown me that there was more to life than marrying a man and having his children. It seemed to me that she'd forgotten the power of love.

"Maria, why would you choose to do this to yourself?" she asked me many times.

"I'm in love, Mother, and I don't want to spend my entire life alone."

"I didn't spend my life alone," she said bitterly. "I was surrounded by people, great people who will make changes in the world."

"I know," I said, trying to console her. I could see she was well on her way to another lecture for me. "But you worked to ensure that we would have a country where we could live in peace and that's what I'm choosing for my life: the very peace that you fought for."

She could hardly argue with me there, because I was correct in all areas. Still, I think she had expected me to have the same ambition she did as a young woman; she was struggling with the idea that her job was done and it was now time for her to rest.

Nevertheless, she made sure to remind my love that he had best not behave like his late father-in-law; those kinds of libertine behaviours were not anymore accepted now than they had been when she was young. Naturally, Ludovico was irritated with such talk and it caused some friction between him and my mother.

"Why does she insist that the sins of the past will be revisited?" he asked me one night after she had gone to bed. She was visiting us in Milan, making the trek out of her retirement to see me.

"She is only worried for us and our baby," I said. I patted my round belly, proof of my legacy. Mother had insisted it was a mistake to have many children, that it wouldn't afford me the life that I truly would want to live.

"Well I'm hardly the same man as he was, and you are not the same woman as she," he groused.

"Let her be, Ludovico. She has little in her life to work toward now, and she needs to feel useful where she can. If trying to protect her family is all she can do, then let her do it."

I often visited with my mother, hoping to make up for the time I spent as a child in resentment; she had siblings, certainly, and I know she visited with them and wrote letters, but I worried that she wasn't socializing enough anymore. Once she had strived to be the very center of attention, and now she only wanted to seclude herself and write.

I have to admit that being with her in that capacity was somewhat disconcerting and tiresome; I longed for the days when crowds would fill our home and mother would host soirees. Those days were now in our past, and the lack of excitement in her future was unsettling.

My mother was no longer the young woman I remembered from my youth. Her injuries had only grown more prominent and seemed to be wearing on her all the more as she aged; it was difficult to watch and I found myself desiring to leave her presence almost as soon as I arrived.

It was easy for me to get caught up in my own family life. Ludovico and I had several children and we were happy enough in Milan. Life was not always easy, but it was far better than the one I had been raised in.

Despite the nuisance my mother could make of herself with my husband, I knew that they too shared a bond, or at the very least an understanding. Eventually she recognized that Ludo was not the fickle man she initially believed he was. Instead, he was a steadfast father and doting husband and I considered myself lucky to have wed him rather than Antonio.

After the unification of Italy, I devoted my time to being a wife and a mother, while my mother still spent hers trying to better the world. She focused on our time in Turkey in particular, having been somewhat traumatized by the way she saw women treated there. In her opinion it was the lack of education in the empire that caused the women to be so accepting of their place in their culture. I wasn't so sure, but I didn't choose to chase that line of thought with my mother; her passion would likely eclipse mine in any case.

I was glad to see that she had taken some time to enjoy retirement, though. She often travelled between Lake Como and Milan, depending on the season and her mood. She was a good grandmother to my children when she was present, but sometimes she wasn't quite present as she thought of the words she wanted to write.

Sometimes I would visit her in Lake Como and I have to say that her life of solitude rather left me with a feeling of ennui. She never did marry again, having such a strong objection to the tradition, and therefore I felt she was lonely. She never admitted as much to me, and I suspect that she still wrote to many friends, but I know that some of them had passed away.

I think she missed François the most; though he hadn't been her husband, he had been her companion and lover, I was now certain, and she wished she had more time with him. Unfortunately, François chose to remain in France where he had set himself up as a journalist and owner of some news publications.

I'm not certain if he was able to visit mother or not, she rarely spoke of those things with me; I suspect the idea that she wanted the presence of a man in her life was something she would have considered to be a weakness more than anything.

I was grateful that she at least had the company of Mary Anne there; my governess had remained in her employ even after I had moved on from being a girl to a woman and the two remained steadfast friends. I feared that if Mary Anne were not with my mother, the only interaction my mother would have at times with humanity would be with her servants.

Our relationship over the years had waxed and waned, and now that she was older, I felt myself drawn to her more than ever. I spent many hours visiting with her as much as I could. Sometimes we painted together, though more often than not, I found that she was more interested in discussing politics with me; it was comforting to think that even in her advanced age she was still a woman with a passion.

I can say with complete honesty that I've never known true anger until I attended my mother's funeral.

She passed away in Milan, and it came as a shock to me. Though I knew her health was waning, part of me was denying that the end of her time was a possibility. In many ways it was, her many letters, essays and books would ensure that her feelings would be heard by many people in the years to come, but it was only a sad echo of who she was.

Ludo and the children did their best to comfort me, but it was something that I felt I must face alone. For most of our lives it had just been the two of us, and now there was only one. Mary Anne was there, of course, but while she was dear to me, she was not my blood, and there could be no replacing my mother.

My family and I arranged a funeral befitting her status as a socialite and patriot who had helped to piece our country together with every fibre of her being.

To my utter disgust not one member of the state, the state that she had helped to create and dedicated the majority of her life to, bothered to attend her funeral. Not one.

Their ungratefulness left a bitter taste in my mouth and dear Ludo had to plead with me to not make more of it than it was. In my anger I wished to attend the offices of some of these gentlemen and shame them. They deserved to know they were cowards and be recognized for using my mother for their own personal gains.

I never did hold as much respect for our fine country after that as I previously had. I'm not sure what my mother would have had to say; I don't think she would like to think that they'd forgotten about her. But perhaps she would only utter an acerbic remark and carry on all the while as though she never expected them to come in the first place; as if she didn't want them to attend and they were doing her the favour.

The death of my mother left me contemplating many things in my world. As a mother myself, I wasn't sure that

I had eclipsed my mother's glory or if I had only fallen into her shadow. My oldest daughter, Maria, and I were not as close as I would have preferred and I wasn't sure how to bridge the gap.

I had spoken to my mother about it, of course, but she had little advice to offer; our situation had been so much different than the one I've had with my children; the circumstances were hardly comparable and I was left to find my own way in the dark.

13

CRISTINA, 1870

Italy

The satisfaction of seeing my hard work around me every day was more than enough for me in my retirement. My efforts had all been worthwhile, as had my sacrifices.

There was only one area in which I wish I had spent more time; and even then I'm not certain it would have had a positive outcome: Maria. She had settled for a life of mundanity, marrying a wealthy man, purportedly for love, but I can't be certain of that, and then having children. Her entire life was about being a mother and a wife; how could she have come from someone like me?

I never did care for Ludovico; I'm certain that he was not as loyal as Maria was led to believe. In the end, I don't believe any man of the type of loyalty that Maria seemed to believe in; they have primal urges that cannot be ignored, even by the most controlled. However, she didn't view the world the way I did and I'm certain she felt the lack of a male in her life strongly.

At least it wasn't Antonio. That brief courtship had been quite worrisome for me; it was only through desperate measures that I was able to convince her of the folly of such a choice. It had pained me to do that to her, but it was a necessity.

I spent time with my grandchildren as every grandmother is obligated to do, but I didn't get much joy from them; they were spoiled and demanded all of Maria's energy, not allowing her an opportunity to explore those things that mattered to her. I dreaded the visits with the children, but I looked forward to time with her alone.

Mary Anne was always better with the children than I was, and I suspect I should be grateful for that; it was likely the only positive experience they really received when they visited me.

I spent my time between Lake Como and Milan, preferring the beauty and retreat of the lake. It reminded me, somewhat, of our time on the farm and Turkey. Those years there had been peaceful, likely the most peaceful that I'd ever experienced, aside from our adventures across the empire.

Those years of my life were the ones I thought about the most, now that I was no longer in quite so much demand politically. Once the men had established the government, they hardly needed me any more, and that was fine with me. Everyone deserves some time to enjoy peace.

However, though I have time for peace, it doesn't mean that I'm required to lay down my pen. As I look around me, I wonder how much progress has really been made during my lifetime. I've seen women in Turkey who will never know what it is like to be free or independent. They will spend their lifetime ignorant of the life they should have if they don't receive the education that they need.

Worse yet, slavery still exists in this world, and it's a subject that I've hardly touched on as I've focused on my country. I see all around me things that need improvement and few people who are calling to action for it. What kind of world was I leaving behind for Maria? Was it truly a better one?

There was no way for me to be certain about any of it, as is the way of life. We can only achieve so much while we are living and breathing and to want more is egocentric.

Given the life I was afforded in this world I have done everything in my power to make it better. I fought against those who wished us to serve them without answering for their power. I advised the people of the options and opportunities they had available to them should they choose to fight.

I raised a girl, on my own, who is doing nothing more than bearing children.

How I wish she had my passion, but even to the end she must prove that she is nothing like me. She is not a woman of Italy, she is a woman of the world, having too many homes to claim one as her only.

Whilst I longed for the nation where I was born and the chance to better it, she longed only for a place to call home; a place where she could truly grow roots and live a life free from the chaos that I brought with me like a whirlwind.

I had to wonder if in my efforts to sculpt her in my likeness, if I instead pushed her away from me. After all, when you are working with clay you have to be gentle and guiding, otherwise you end up creating something you had no desire for. Sometimes, those are the most beautiful of creations.

To the rest of the world, the one that I couldn't touch or affect in any reality, I was leaving behind my thoughts; a piece of myself that would hopefully one day bring on the change the world needed.

For my daughter, the best I could hope was that I left her with an example of a woman who stood for what she believed in and the memory of love.

Dear Caroline,

> *I was glad to see your letter the other day, and I'm happy to hear that you are doing well. I myself have been puttering away writing essays and books, hoping to ensure the world of tomorrow is better than the world of today.*

> *I'm slowing down, now. Since the attempted murder on my life, I have not been the same woman. The fire and passion still brims inside me, but my body no longer responds the way it used to, and I'm*

afraid it has seemed to give me a bit of a diminutive stature, which I'm certain affects the way people view me.

I do my best to hide it from Maria, but I'm certain she can see it and is saddened by it. I'm not the woman she grew up with, not physically anyway. I've retained my wit, something I hope to keep until my dying day.

I do have to confess that I see a difference in my daughter as well. When she was but a child I had such hopes and desires for her life; I imagined her to be a fierce warrior of human rights, one who was raised to see the wrongs in the world and then fix those same wrongs. Instead, she is content to bear children and make her husband happy, a life I would never have chosen for her.

It hurts me to watch her lose touch with the realities around her and to accept the limitations that are forced upon her and her own children. She should be pushing the boundaries, showing her children that bettering the world is the only way to live. Instead, the mundanity of her life is astounding.

*I find myself dreading her visits on more and
more occasions; do not mistake my love
for my daughter, because it is fierce, but I
find that when she comes to visit she has
nothing interesting to say because she has
done nothing of note. The years of babies
was arduous to me because hardly
another subject crossed her tongue. Worse
still was her expectation of me to be the
grandmotherly type she'd always wanted.
She should know better, you would think;
I was never the mother she wanted me to
be either.*

*I wonder, is this a conundrum that all
mothers must face at some point? The
utter disappointment when your child
does not become the person you were
molding them to be feels sharper than
any knife wound I've experienced. I do
not want to be dissatisfied with my
daughter's choices, but I struggle with
seeing how I could possibly embrace
them.*

*She is living a life showing that she is quite
content with the status quo, one that she
knows had to be fought for. I had hoped
she would ride on the waves of my success
and make further changes in the world
around her, but I believe she will not be*

a woman that history remembers, which is a shame.

Looking back I can only wish I had been more persuasive when trying to convince her not to marry. One doesn't need a husband to feel content or whole in life, I dare say that even a child cannot necessarily offer it to a woman, though Heaven knows society likes to tell us that it is.

I wonder, Caroline, if the fault does not lie with me. Perhaps I pushed her too hard and rather than try to be like me she strove to be the exact opposite. Well, in that I'm being too harsh, she is not the opposite of me, to be certain, but she is definitely very different from me and I don't think she will accomplish the same things in her life that I have done.

In many ways, I was perhaps too much a mother to Italy and not enough to my own flesh and blood. Because of that, I fear my legacy does not lie with my daughter's future, but with the words I write, and it may only be those future readers who ever remember me.

I apologize for the melancholy sound of my

*letter, it seems that as the years move
forward I become more retrospective and
look toward those that have already been
passed by.*

*I value our friendship and the advice you've
given me over the years, and I hope that
I've bestowed upon you the same gifts I
have received.*

Sincerely,
Cristina

14

MARIA, 1899

Rome

"Madame, your visitor, he is here. A Mario Esposito," said the maid.

"Let him in," I said with a sigh.

The time had come, though my mother was largely forgotten since her death, for others to wish to immortalize her memory. They sought to do so using mine; after all, who could possibly have a better insight?

The gentlemen entered my drawing room with an air of eagerness, he was young and I could see that he was eager to make a name for himself off of the back of my mother's. His only tools were pencils and paper. He offered me a brief bow as he entered and I waved a hand at him dismissing the gesture; it was my mother who was the princess, not me. Such gestures were unnecessary in this modern world; we were looking at a new century.

"Madame," he said and I waved again.

"Please, call me Maria. I tire of all of the titles and

formality. If I'm to tell you the complete truth of my mother, then I must be somewhat casual with you, true?"

"Of course… Maria." He seemed to struggle with my name on his tongue, but I refused to renege and would not answer to anything else.

When I had first been approached by this man I had declined without any consideration. Though I felt this was something my mother would want for herself, I was tired of being thought of only in regard to my relationship with her. No one cared to hear the accomplishments of my life.

Unfortunately, the subject brought forth some feelings of nostalgia and I found myself reading some of her letters and paging through some of her books, finding her old essays that had been published in numerous papers.

I was rarely mentioned in a positive light; I fear that I was her greatest challenge until the end, though we did get along. She had wanted more for me, as I suspect every mother wants for their child. I, too, was guilty of such fancies.

"Can I assume you've done some research?" I asked, perhaps a little more forward than I should have been. I wasn't entirely comfortable with this situation just yet.

He didn't seem to take offense, instead he only nodded enthusiastically. "I didn't bring my notes with me, nor my books, but if you'd like I can bring them next time."

The reminder that this was to be the first of several meetings was already tedious. "Can I offer you a drink?" I asked, standing and making my way to a cabinet that stood stocked at the side of the room.

I pulled out two glasses and opened the ice box,

clinking several chunks into my own. "Yes, please," he said.

I didn't give him an option on the beverage, instead I poured us each some scotch on ice and sat down again. Difficult times called for stiff drinks, and this little rendezvous was not going to be easy.

"Where shall we start?"

"Well, as I said M-Maria, I have done my research, so I have a basic understanding of the biography of your mother. She was born in 1808 to Girolamo Trivulzio and the Vittoria dei Marchesi Gherardini. Her father passed away when she was twelve and her mother eventually remarried to Alessandro Visconti d'Aragona…"

He carried on, naming all of my aunts and uncles, who they married, etcetera. His research was quite in depth, so I was fairly certain there would be few corrections on my part.

As he named all of these people to whom I was related, though, I realized that they were for the most part strangers to me. Though my mother shared stories of them with me, and I can only assume stories of me with them, I never spent a significant amount of time with any of them.

There was always only my mother; my world had revolved around her desires and her impulses. Perhaps that was the reason that I'd chosen such a predictable life; it was something I'd never had.

He looked at me expectantly, narrow blue eyes open as wide as they could and bushy blond eyebrows raised. I tried to recall his last words but they weren't there. "I do apologize, sir, all these memories seem to have made my mind wander. Could you please repeat the question?"

I expected him to be offended—I would have been—but instead his expression only grew curious. "I was just checking the accuracy of my information with you, but perhaps..." he licked his lips, a nasty habit, I thought, then started again, "perhaps you wouldn't mind sharing your thoughts with me?"

"My thoughts?"

"Yes, were you thinking about your mother?"

Of course I was, he would have to be a dimwit to think otherwise and I wished to tell him so. However, politeness reigned in my tone and I answered his question honestly. "Yes, I was thinking about her."

"What exactly, if you don't mind?" He had started writing words on his paper without looking down at his notepad. The entirety of his attention, with the exception of his moving hand, was on me.

"Well, I suppose I was thinking how very different our lives ended up being."

"Ah yes, you've lived a life out of the spotlight. You've mostly spent your time with your family, whereas your mother was quite the socialite, bringing delight wherever she travelled."

"As opposed to me?" I asked, my tone was icy.

He had the good grace to blush as he realized his blunder. "No, I wouldn't presume... I just meant to say that your mother was someone who sought out attention, whereas you seem to do quite the opposite."

He was correct there, I'd done everything I could to avoid being the center of attention. If ever Ludovico was called upon for any social events, I did my best to stay in his shadow and allow him to shine, I'd stood out enough in my lifetime. "My mother sought out the attention of others because she had an agenda, Mario. Her charm wasn't a natural, guileless gift, it was a tool she sharpened whenever she had the opportunity.

"I, however, did not have an agenda or underlying desire to force anything on to others during my lifetime. My only desire was to live happily with my family."

He nodded, still moving his hand along the paper. Part of me wished I could see what he was writing, what he felt was so important in my words, but I tamped down the desire. That part of me was like Mother, at least, I detested showing any vulnerability and to show interest would suggest that I was insecure about his words.

"Can you tell me a bit about your childhood?"

"It was chaotic," I said. "As my mother's actions had her on the run, she drug me along with her. I had no choice except to follow."

"But it must have been somewhat exciting, seeing history acted out before you," he said with a wistful smile.

"It wasn't history at the time. It was my life and I can't say there was much to be excited about."

He blushed again and nodded. "That is true, so it's safe to say that your mother's choice of a life didn't agree with you?"

I didn't like where he was going with this; I felt I was being trapped with my own words. So, I sat back and thought carefully about what I was going to say next.

"I don't think that my mother's life agreed with being a mother," I said finally. "She was nomadic, but always wishing to be home. She was so passionate about her plans that sometimes she forgot about me, it seemed. Whenever she had the urge, she would uproot me from my life and take me along on her adventures, regardless of my feelings in the matter. In some cases we were in real danger and I did spend a good deal of my childhood fearful of something happening to me or to her."

"Are you referring to the incident where she was stabbed?" he asked.

"I'm referring to several different incidents, but yes, I suppose that would be one of them. We were refugees much of the time, and when we weren't we were revolutionaries. Neither of those lifestyles has much security in it."

My response seemed to take him askance, and for the first time he looked at his paper with a frown. "I hadn't considered her life in that light," he said finally. "How do you feel about your life now, knowing what you do?"

"I'm not sure I understand your question," I said. I did understand, it was one that I was asked often and I truly hoped that he had intelligence enough to posit a different one to me.

"I mean, now, as a mother, how do you feel your mother did, given all of her circumstances, some of which were out of her control?"

He did have intelligence, and I could see by the gleam in his eyes that he knew I'd been testing his merit.

The question was a valid one, and one that I hadn't really considered myself. I'd spent many years of my life either running as fast as I could from my mother or running toward her only to find her distracted by something else, something she deemed to be more important than me.

Still, looking back on my own experiences as a mother, I can see how she would have been tested with my attitude from time to time. Lord knows I'd struggled with my own children and their fits of fury and I was dedicated to being their mother. Perhaps it is the nature of a mother and her child to struggle, perhaps it is that very struggle that ensures continuity of the species, forcing the next generation to always adapt.

His question brought forth an uncomfortable feeling in me as I was reminded of my own struggles with my daughter, Maria. She was very much like her grandmother, I have to say, always flitting around from here to there with her mind filled with ideas. I had tried to ground her and to keep her safe, but that effort had not worked in my favour. We had barely spoken in years, exchanging a letter only at Christmas, and even that was short and terse.

"I can say for certain," I said after a moment of silence, "that she was not ever intentionally cruel or malicious. She only ever wanted the best for me. Looking back, I would think that we just had two very different ideas about what was best for me."

"So you would say that she was a good mother?"

"I would say that she was as good a mother as could be expected, given the choices she had made before I came along."

"Do you have any memories that you wish to share?"

I was struck by an insistent urge to open up to Mario, one that I tried to deny because I was afraid I would look weak.

"When we fled Italy, her for the second time, me for the first, she was kind enough to bring along our governess, Mary Anne Parker. I imagine that it was quite expensive to smuggle a third person out of the country, but I believe she did it so that I might have a little bit of stability during the tumultuous time." Though I'd spoken from the heart, his hand didn't stop moving and he didn't stop listening, urging me to continue on silently.

"I had never been on a boat until we fled the country. It was an unnerving experience for me, especially given the conditions we had to travel in; one is rarely in luxurious settings when being smuggled from a country. During our time on the boat, she was always at my side, comforting me with soft words and reassurances that everything was going to be fine.

"And it was; there were times of struggle, certainly, but in the end everything went just as she had hoped it would, right down to the Italian States uniting."

He had that wistful look on his face again. "If you could say something to your mother right now, what would it be?"

Again, his question took me by surprise. Certainly I had talked to my mother after she passed, I'm certain that all daughters are inclined to do so. Our mothers are the source of our knowledge, if we don't ask them questions we'll never know how to navigate in the world.

"I would tell her that she was right," I said finally.

"Right?" he asked. "About what?"

"Everything."

Thankfully our interview was completed shortly afterward. He asked me some more questions about certain events, but I suspect that he already knew the answers and was only looking for my perspective. I wasn't sure what kind of biography he could be writing that my opinion mattered so much, but I was grateful for the opportunity to think about my life again.

After he left, promising to return in the next couple of days with a fresh crop of questions, I poured myself another drink. I looked over to my writing desk, neat and tidy in a way that my mother's never was. Was my tidiness something I'd developed as a balance to her chaos?

I thought of Maria, my own daughter who had done everything in her power to become something altogether different than I had. She was in America, now, a country that could be considered older than Italy, but did not have the aged culture that we had in Europe.

With a sigh, I made my way over to my desk and set down my glass before picking up my fountain pen and putting it to paper. Somehow, I felt that I owed my daughter an apology for my own part in our rift. After all, isn't a mother required to forgive and forget regardless of the sin?

Dear Maria,

> *I have received a visitor today, a man, Mario Esposito, who is currently drafting a biography about your grandmother. It was a queer experience to sit with a stranger and confide my childhood thoughts to him, and the interview we had today has me reviewing my life with a critical eye.*

I write to you today with an apology. I fear that I have not always agreed with you on what was the best decision for you to make with your life, and I must say that it was likely not up to me to decide what was best for you.

My own mother and I had a tumultuous relationship at times, one that only survived its ups and downs because she stubbornly insisted upon it. I know that she didn't always agree with my choice to marry and have children rather than pursue some greater calling.

To this day, many years after her death, I disagree with her; creating a family with your father was the best decision I made, and I wouldn't ask for any other. Because of her character, I don't believe that's something that she would ever have understood.

She had fought her entire life to give Italy stability, and in the end, she struggled to live a quiet life herself, having lost herself to the warrior woman of freedom. I, however, saw what she had fought for and succeeded in getting, and decided that I would indeed enjoy that peace, and in fact, glory in it.

*How very odd that her goal for her country,
her true passion, would turn out to be the
one thing that caused her the most
frustration in the end?*

*I fear that my intentions with you, my
daughter, can also be skewed in such a
way. Perhaps, knowing the childhood
that I grew up with, I struggled against
your creativity and insistence on running
rather than walking because I was afraid
it would lead you to a life similar to
what I experienced. I can't say that I can
look back and have many fond memories
of my childhood.*

*What I can say, with confidence, is that while
I was certain that my mother was only
fighting for her own selfish intentions, I
was incorrect. My mother was trying to
give me a life that she couldn't have, one
that she felt would offer me the best
chances of success. Our thoughts on that
direction may not have always aligned,
but they were always working hand in
hand.*

*As I spoke to Mario today, and he asked me
to recall fond memories of my mother, I
realized that I had to struggle to think of
any. It occurred to me during that time*

*that you must invariably feel the same of
me, otherwise I suspect our relationship
would be more cordial.*

*I do not believe in perfection, it's an
impossible standard, there is always room
for improvement—a sentiment your
grandmother would heartily agree with.
Therefore, I know that I was not always
the best mother for you. There were
certainly times that I was not there in the
way that you needed me to be, and, my
dear Maria, I am sorry for that.*

*I know that we have our differences, but I
have to say that again, I do not wish to
be like my mother. In the end she was
disappointed in my life choices, I believe,
and I hated feeling that I disappointed
her.*

*You are not a disappointment to me, my
darling. You are the wild and carefree
grandchild of a woman who changed the
world. And for that, I will forever be
grateful.*

*Sincerely,
Your mother.*

Made in the USA
Middletown, DE
05 April 2021

37058189R00116